From The Women's Press Ltd
34 Great Sutton Street, London EC1V 0DX

Mary Jones was born in India, but grew up and was educated in England. She has had a variety of jobs: private secretary to a national newspaper proprietor; hostess on a cruise liner; free-lance writing and managing a herbal-tea firm as well as running her own antiques business. She has a grown-up daughter and lives in London with their three dogs.

For some years she was a member of the Al-Anon Family Groups and is at present a counsellor with Cruse, the National Organisation for the Bereaved.

All royalties accruing from the sale of this book will be donated to the Marie Curie Memorial Foundation for research on pain control.

MARY JONES

Secret Flowers

Mourning and the adaptation to loss

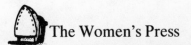 The Women's Press

Published by the Women's Press Limited 1988
A member of the Namara Group
34 Great Sutton Street, London EC1V 0DX

British Library Cataloguing in Publication Data available

The lines from 'The Hollow Men' by T.S. Eliot are reprinted from *Collected Poems 1909–1962* (Faber & Faber, 1942) with the publisher's permission.

Typeset by MC Typeset Limited, Chatham, Kent
Printed and bound in Great Britain by Cox & Wyman Ltd, Reading, Berks.

To Anne, with all my love

'Grief work consists of:

1 Experiencing the reality of the death;
2 Feeling the pain;
3 Adjusting to life without the deceased;
4 Saying goodbye and building a new life.

These are the four tasks of mourning.'

Counsellors' Training Programme,
Cruse, the National Organisation for the Bereaved

O! While you live, tell truth
and shame the Devil.

William Shakespeare

King Henry IV, Part I

I have been so nervous, writing this – a snail without a shell, an elephant lumbering over quicksands. Lost and insecure, my courage failed me a hundred times. I slipped and floundered. Once, as you will see, I crawled on hands and knees in the mud.

But I did pick myself up. In the end, I can lift my chin and say, 'But I kept on. I was faithful. I was true to the best that was in ourselves.'

*

If I could still talk to my husband, I wonder, now, what he would say of my writing this. I do not think he would approve. He would object from habit, from caution, and then say, maddeningly, 'But you must do as you think best.'

Only now do I realise how much I like my own way, and I would argue. I should say, 'Do you remember when my father died? How upset I was? You were so good: you listened, and that helped me through the early grief. Did you know it was one of your great strengths? You were the only person I have ever met who made listening into a positive act. I sometimes thought that was why you were such a good journalist, people talked to you. And each night you listened as I talked out all my feelings, hour after hour. Afterwards, when I met a lively, laughing mind and attraction sparkled in my eye, I turned away from temptation, shut off the current, remembered how good you were, that I "owed" you. I never told you. I was married to you, and I was too shy!

'You were someone who, when you met a person in trouble, went further down the road with them than anyone else. I used to watch you doing this, and I was cross because people drained you and made you so tired. I never said anything, because you did the same for me. It was your nature; an impatient, intolerant man who was capable of an excess of patience and tolerance, who found loving difficult yet had an enormous capacity to love.

'Now, I have to face your death. You, who were so close to me, have crossed that terrifying, unknown border we shall all cross. Part of me has gone too, a coat belt caught in a slammed door. I am amputated and alone. You are the only person in the world who could really help me, now, to get over your death, and you're not here. So, I must stumble and limp. I must just do the best I can.'

*

Death is universal, so everyone must experience loss. By their forties, most people know someone close to them who has died. Death releases a host of strong emotions, not expected. We do not talk about them, nor write about them, so there are few guidelines to warn how you will feel, nothing charted, little to help. I was totally unprepared for all the things that happened, and when they did I was amazed, surprised and utterly devastated. Nothing like this had ever happened to me before, so I had no experience on which to fall back.

My father died after a brief illness. I was his only child, and we adored each other, so my loss was tremendous. I wept and wept, and went on weeping occasionally for a year or two. My mother's death was peaceful and anticipated. My aunt, to whom we were all close, with whom I worked and who was part of our daily life, dropped down dead one morning; a dreadful shock and loss.

So, I was no stranger to mourning. But no past experience bore any relation to the devastation I now felt. It was as if all the sorrows I had ever known were scribbles on the corner of rough paper, screwed up and thrown away, beside this grief.

*

I have today made a promise. I have put a new ribbon in my typewriter and when it grows faint, I shall stop writing. If a famous author* limited himself to four notebooks, I shall trust him, follow his example.

As long as I live I shall probably grieve, even if time makes it more gentle, less frequent. But in death and grief, because there is pain, therefore I know there is life, and life is change and I must set some limit or I shall nibble at these thoughts and feelings for the rest of my life.

I tried to begin to write this several times. The words would not come and I felt self-conscious and unhappy. Then, two things happened within a few days.

A woman stopped me outside my house and asked if I were the lady who had just lost her husband. 'My Alf died in March,' she said, eyeing me fiercely, adding, 'I can't cry. Crying won't bring him back.' I looked at her elderly, work-worn face and said, 'Perhaps that isn't the point of crying.'

Then she told me what Alf had said, just before he died, as he held her hand. Almost identical words had been said to me. We were two women and both knew we were special, chosen and lucky. It was so simple, so mundane; we had been given deep love by another human being, whom we had

*C.S. Lewis, *A Grief Observed*.

3

loved in return. As we parted, she added, militant, daring me to laugh: 'I still say good-night to him, every night.' 'So do I.' It didn't seem odd to be standing in the street, talking to a woman whose name I did not even know then, saying things I have not told to my closest friends. We were neither of us shy, it was perfectly natural.

A few days later, I went to a meeting run by counsellors specialising in the problems of bereavement. I was irritated and at variance with most of the chairman's talk, but in closing the meeting he spoke again: 'You will have come here for many different reasons, and you will have listened to many different things. When you go home, there will be one word you will remember. Share that word.'

That is all I can remember – share. Because I have the gift of words, I speak for those who do not. There is nothing at all special in my grief and in my feelings. It is only unique in the sense that my fingerprints are unique, and that what was created between Stanley and me was unique and personal. To share eliminates the dreadful isolation, makes happiness and, best of all, makes death utterly, totally meaningless.

*

When I arranged my husband's funeral, and I gave a great deal of thought to it – I wanted it to be something he would have enjoyed – and it was full of meaning, custom-built for him, I thought it was my last act of love. Now, I find I am wrong, and I shall do many other acts of love. I thought all sorts of things, but my thoughts did not seem to have any rational basis and I did not trust them. I knew what I felt, but my feelings were so confused, I did not trust them either.

The word 'widow' derives from the Latin word meaning 'empty'. In my emptiness there was only confusion. I could not hold an idea, want to do something, for more than a few minutes. I, who had hitherto dealt easily with my finances,

4

run a business, looked after a home, had always been confident and competent, was so totally full of insecurity and doubt I could hardly cross the road alone.

Every tiny difficulty was a huge problem. Parking by the shop is not easy. I used to wake up in the morning, and my first thought was anxious: dread that I wouldn't be able to find somewhere to leave the car, and what would I do? It got so bad that I thought I would have to avoid the whole issue; walk or take a taxi. I was so ashamed of these feelings, I have never brought myself to tell anyone, just secreted them away inside myself.

*

I seem to have come to know and understand my husband better since his death, and I find this odd and surprising. Random remarks by our friends were suddenly illuminating, and I recognised characteristics of which I was previously hardly aware. I had never thought about them, because I was always involved in feeling. I did not need to think because our relationship was always there, instant and accessible, a fast underground river that our tempestuous surface life did not affect.

Perhaps that is what love is, a deep bond, independent of our will, often of our happiness or comfort, that endured. Not only in a lifetime, though that spanned nearly thirty years, more than half my life, but lasting now, as I write, with a presence still which makes it a great happiness to be alone.

Years ago, a friend from early youth said of him: 'For you, he is the abiding one.' Now that the torment of the early grief has gone – although I never thought it would go – I feel enormously enriched. I had always agreed that 'to know and love one other human being is the root of all wisdom',* but

*Evelyn Waugh, *Brideshead Revisited*.

my early mourning pushed knowledge further, and I understood Ecclesiastes: 'In much wisdom is much grief'. No doubt, for many people with a direct and straightforward relationship, grief is simple. I was like a widow who said: 'He was a bad-tempered bugger all his life, but I loved him.'

*

There were things about his dying, and his death, that surprised me. One was how quietly but definitely death announces itself, so that deep down I recognised it from afar.

Stanley was ill in early December. He was a bronchitic. We were all used to him not being well in the winter, used to his chest infections. He responded eventually to the antibiotics, but by New Year's Eve I knew, without knowing how, almost without knowing that I did know, that it would be his last.

Nine months before, our daughter had her eighteenth birthday, and we had a big party. Someone asked me why we celebrated that anniversary rather than her twenty-first and apparently I said, 'Because her father won't be alive then,' although afterwards, when it was repeated to me, I had no memory of saying it, no conscious knowledge it was to be true.

And in the early months of that year, as he grew more and more unwell and yet still would not go to the chest clinic as the doctor had ordered, I behaved exactly as if I knew Stanley would die so soon. I wrote to my eldest stepson in New Zealand, a warning letter: 'if you can come back, do come sooner rather than later . . . I don't want you afterwards to feel excluded, that you didn't know . . .' After a week or two, I wrote to my second stepson in the country, the same kind of letter. I rang up Stanley's previous wife: She knew about the violent quarrel with the third son, and I said, 'If anything happens, he'll feel so bad if they haven't made up,' and he came at once, with his younger brother. Each came to see his father quietly and alone, and I left the men together, I had no place there. Yet we had no idea what was the matter, that Stanley's life was measured only in weeks.

I behaved exactly as I would have done had I been given the terrible and exact medical diagnosis the young doctor at the hospital was to give me six weeks later.

*

I was more surprised to find how sexual is death. I now understand how a person whose partner is dying might, in some circumstances, go out and couple violently and casually. It would neither shock nor startle me, yet I might have lived all my life without this knowledge.

Almost immediately Stanley went into hospital, I went out and bought new clothes; a pretty blouse, some knickers. When I went to visit in hospital, I always wore careful make-up, put on my expensive but familiar scent, took a comb in my pocket for final running repairs; always wore clean pants, and recognised an 'in-case-I-might-take-them-off' feeling. For a few days I went with the same high excitement I had known when Stanley and I first met. I said to him, 'I feel like a girl again; the twenty-two hours until I next see you are just wasted time, to be lived through.'

Somehow, I knew I had felt all these things before, recognised them, but I never identified them until I was telling a young married woman of our acquaintance. She looked at me, tears in her eyes, and said, 'Don't you know? You were courting!' And that was it. I could have been eighteen again, going to meet a new lover, not an over-weight, distraught, middle-aged woman visiting her dying husband.

In the ward, there was another woman who, like me, had open visiting hours because our husbands were so ill. I

7

looked over to her, saw she was wearing tight black trousers and a scarlet silk blouse. I recognised party dress. 'You too!' I thought.

*

When I knew Stanley was going to die, when the doctor said, 'He has a wild, untreatable tumour. There is nothing we can do, and he will die very soon,' I made three decisions. Perhaps decisions is not quite the right word, that implies consideration and there was no time to consider. But I instantly felt I must hold to three things: I must be as unchanged and normal as possible; I must try to make him laugh and I must not cry in front of him. What I really knew passionately was that Stanley should live, right up to the moment that he died; that he should share our life, be a part of the pulsing, sunlit action.

The hospital bed was now his only home. I must take to it as much normality as I could. Without previous thought, I instantly accepted the truth of the doctor's comment: 'Your husband is a very brave man.' The only honour and love I could bring now was to meet this courage exactly and in my own way.

I was one person who could always make him laugh. We were a couple with apparently nothing in common. After-wards, people said, 'I don't know how you two ever got together or stayed together.' Nor did I. We differed on religion, on politics, on finance. We came from totally different social backgrounds, I a cavalry officer's daughter, he a taxi driver's son. We had turned into unexpectedly different people, considering our start in life; he a journalist working for the national press, and I an antique dealer working in a market. We loved our daughter – and we liked the way the other loved her. We loved our home, and each other. I used to say, 'I'm not the right wife for you, you

8

should have married someone who's interested in the things you care about. You know they mean very little to me.' Yet I had for him this one gift of laughter.

He might be furiously angry with me, but he was never bored. And when a situation became too intense, the emotion too tight, I could defuse it. I can hear him saying, with a wry grin preceding reluctant laughter, 'You are a bitch!' He was the only person I have ever known who was not afraid of what he called my 'mordant tongue'. Even when I was at my most acid, I made him laugh because he knew there was love, too, under the words. After Stanley's death, when I sat and thought – because there was not much else I could be bothered to do – I realised that we had given each other, for safe-keeping, some dark part of our own natures that made us alarmed and ashamed. When I made a 'flip' remark, he only laughed and enjoyed the well-turned phrase and the speed of my mind. Although his powerful and overbearing personality sometimes made me afraid, we both knew he could never make me do something I knew was wrong. So we kept each other safe. Long afterwards, a colleague visited me and said of him, 'A clever man, but very moody and difficult too, yet he always enjoyed a good laugh.' Then I knew what I had given him, how he must have valued it.

Shortly after he went into hospital, it was my birthday. Our daughter made a cake, we took it in to the ward, I cut, wished. We were just there, together; three of us, a small, ordinary family marking a commonplace family ritual, and with no feeling 'This is the last time.' The thought never crossed my mind. We simply practised one of the Alcoholics Anonymous prayers: 'Look well into today, for today is life'.

So, that vow I kept. I kept the other, too, and I quarrelled with him all through the six weeks he had left to live. After all, that was the norm; obsequious agreement would have struck a false note indeed! Often his behaviour was so impossible, I threatened to walk out. When he swore at me, I said, 'I won't be spoken to like that! I shall leave!' This was

9

unfair, because I could leave the ward and he could not. And I don't think I would have walked out; in any case, I never did, although once or twice I would have been justified.

And the third vow I broke only once, that I would not cry in front of him. I should hate to be visited by someone who wept, but one afternoon I sat by his bed and held his hand when we both knew he was going to die, very soon, days possibly, certainly within a few weeks, and I said: 'I've run out of courage this afternoon, and I'll have to borrow some of yours.'

Now, I am glad I did cry, because he might not have known how much I cared, I might have seemed indifferent. Perhaps it helped him, too; by giving me good heart he reinforced his own. Certainly it was normal to turn to him for comfort in distress, to seek reassurance.

*

Some people asked directly, with others it was unspoken; soon, I found it better to say it first, 'Yes, he did know he was going to die.' The doctor told us both, separately; a wild tumour, untreatable. That young man's honesty and courage were, and still are, of the most incalculable help. It was not easy for him, trained to save life, and to find himself helpless. To me, then, he was just a man, authority in a white coat. It was only afterwards I realised how young he was.

He made himself available to all of us; the children went to see him, talked alone to him. I wrote to him, and his reply, full of insecurity and doubts, made me want to put my arms round him: 'I didn't know how to approach you and Stanley and Anne, I didn't know how to cope with you all.' I would never have guessed; he was clean and true and honest and compassionate. As Stanley said of him, on the first evening of admission, 'That is a good man.' I was surprised by that rare and high accolade from my ruthlessly critical husband.

10

Realising my own response to the doctor, I took him as my model. I told everyone: 'We are a family in bad trouble. Stanley is going to die, very soon.' And everyone we knew opened their hearts to me, responded with simplicity and love.

I felt as if I walked round with a handful of jewels in my pocket, and to each person I met I gave one, and that gift was a small shift in their heart, a break in their voice, a tear in their eye. It happened time and time again; with tough and unsentimental journalists; my dear friends and my business acquaintances. There were no barriers in 'doing the thing that is right and speaking the truth from the heart'.

We were surrounded by odd coincidences. That first evening, the doctor looked at the notes and said to us: 'I see your family doctor is Dr K. – are you attended by the elder or the younger? My sister trained with the son.' We gave him news of the son who had recently left the practice to work abroad. At once, the situation was friendly and personal; there was no fear of the huge, remote institution all hospitals must be.

Within a week, a woman walked into my shop, recommended by a mutual friend, and we chatted and laughed together. The second time she came, I found she knew another of my customers, also a doctor in the hospital where Stanley was a patient. This doctor, it turned out, was the brother-in-law of Stanley's young houseman. Friends knew his parents; the link went on and on, like tarred string running between beacon fires, and I was encircled by an invisible chain of people who all had connections with each other and with us.

Since Stanley died, I have never seen nor spoken to any one of them again.

In the antique market, my friends and neighbours would look up and smile as I opened for business each week, and I could report, 'Up and down, but OK.' Then came the inevitable Saturday when I had to say, 'No, he didn't make it through the week.' That, of course, was very hard. There is no good way to break bad news. But at least I never felt people were afraid to talk to me, must whisper in corners. Matters were open, and we were surrounded by a great circle of loving comfort.

*

At the time, it didn't strike me as difficult. It is only now, as I write, that I wonder just how we made conversation in those last few weeks. Hospital visiting with someone you live with, and know so well that usually you don't bother to talk to them, is always odd, a little abnormal.

I took him little anecdotes; funny remarks, verbal horrors from the media – always a rich source and particularly appealing to a professional writer. It wasn't difficult at all, even knowing he would die so soon, but I cannot say why not. It only grew hard later, and even that had its own in-built solution. The cancers spread to the brain and, because of the side effects of the drugs, too, he could not talk properly. The palsies increased and he could not feed himself, so I went in at meal times, twice a day, and helped him to eat. It was basic in our relationship that we eat together. If one or the other were late home, we almost always waited for each other for our evening meal. So, we still shared the food time, and we did what people always do in hospital; we watched other people.

*

One day, he said: 'I hope you find someone else.' I said it was unlikely. I told our daughter, so that she should know if I do, I am not disloyal. Living in a household where there was fidelity, she was shocked. Several times later, she asked me if I thought I would marry again, find another. I told her, 'I could never marry someone without a deep commitment to them, not like mine to Dad because that wouldn't be possible, but deep, and I don't think I could ever give that commitment because I couldn't risk this again, I couldn't chance being a widow a second time.' I said, 'I'm too full of Dad. Anyone else would have to get to know him very well in me, and I don't suppose another man would want to do that.'

It was not until then that I understood that our relationship had such a deep basis; that it had always been a case of 'O whistle, and I'll come to you, my lad'. I do not see that death has changed this in any way. But Stanley is no longer alive, so I can never prove nor disprove this, and unless I was certain I should feel I were short-changing any other man. I would have to know that, even in theory only, were Stanley to come and call me I could stand my ground and say, 'I'm sorry, no. I loved you, but now I have a new commitment, other loyalties . . .'

It may be that in a year, two or five years, I shall read these words and laugh at them, but I do not think so.

*

Only one person apart from the family visited Stanley in hospital. His wife is my close friend, but the men had never got on very well. Stanley had been so ill the day before that I had been called to the hospital at breakfast time, and I tried to stop the planned visit. By a series of mishaps I could not do so, but the meeting was a great success. Stanley had rallied and the friend solved the problem of what to talk about in his own way: he and Stanley spent a happy half-hour discussing the funerals of all the mutual friends they had attended recently! The wife was incoherent with indignation and apologies on the telephone that evening. I just laughed; it didn't matter, and in fact had helped.

*

The previous months had been difficult. Stanley would not follow the doctor's instructions and go for an X-ray. The doctor would not come to see him again until this was done, and Stanley grew so ill and grey, more sick each day.

I felt I was being crushed between two ruthless wills, and remarkably unpleasant it was, too.

All life is change; either a threat or a challenge, and now I know death is the same, indistinguishable and therefore not separate and absolute, only another part of the whole.

I had to abstract myself, to become solitary but without anger and resentment, before I could realise that not I but the inner tensions of the situation would resolve the conflict. I must wait, and prepare myself, plan how to act when the time came – as it did – and the problem was resolved.

But it was very hard. I now think Stanley knew what was the matter with him, but it was not an easy thing to have to sit and watch. It is difficult to let another person live their own life, far harder to let them die in their own way.

Our friends repeated Stanley's remark: 'I've given her a hard time these last few months.' I knew he had understood, and the oblique apology comforted me.

His funeral was the only thing we never really discussed, although we could have done so. I just told him, 'We'll sing "Joe Hill" for you.' He knew what I meant. He was never a person for whom you had to dot the Is and cross the Ts. His quick, alert brain had already put the full stop at the end of your next paragraph.

*

14

And what do you talk about when you visit a man who is dying, who may not live another week, may go in a day, may last a month? Stanley made it easier, as ever, because he was so much braver than I. He said, openly, 'You know I'm going to die, don't you?' Twice I dodged it: 'We're all going to die, some just do it sooner than later.' But the third time I met his courage: 'Yes. Do you mind?' He said, 'No.' I believed him. I still believe him. There was nothing more to say.

He asked me, 'What do you think life's all about?' I don't know – and I don't know anyone who does. I could only tell him what I thought: it's the doing that matters, not the obtaining. I looked at him in mismatched hospital pyjamas, with a catheter and bedsores. The bank balance was important before. It would be later, but it was irrelevant now. But the fun and laughter as we had battled together had made us the sum total of the two people we were then, unimportant to anyone else, immensely so to each other.

He reviewed his life with habitual gloom. I did not have to think, from my heart the words came true: 'You have five children, all intelligent and healthy, not in any trouble. You've worked hard all your life and never shirked a responsibility. You have principles, and you have been true to them. You've bettered society, maybe only in tiny ways, by your work and your beliefs. You are sober and you will die sober. What more can anyone ask?'

*

And then the talking ended. Or, rather, it changed, because by then the cancers had reached so much of his brain, causing fits, and the suppressant drugs made him hallucinate.

I visited him at lunch time and in the evening, every day. He always recognised me. Sometimes, he was normal, would kiss me affectionately, chat about mundane things. A few hours later, all this could have changed. His diction was

15

perfect, his logic unimpaired, but I had no idea what he was talking about. He was in a private, shattered world, and I had not been issued with a vocabulary book for his language.

Even in drunken or delirious ramblings there is a clue as to what is on that person's mind. Here, there was nothing. The brain was fractured. He was unable to convey the thought, although it seemed to him as if he had. I could not even guess. It made no sense.

All my life, I have lived closely with animals, and I know speech is not necessary for communication. You need it to convey thought forms, but not to show love.

I had been married for many years to a highly intelligent, verbal and articulate man and he had moulded me by his authority, and he was one who understood both words and the feelings and motives under the words. Now, when he talked to me, I had to guess – and I was not always very successful – what he was trying to say. It was so very ironic; it seemed as if the Fates had produced a particularly clever form of cruelty and were tempting me to hate them, and that anger and hatred would only destroy me.

When I failed to understand, as I inevitably did, Stanley would, naturally, grow violently impatient and angry, and he was frightening. I had to try to put my fear on one side and to concentrate on reducing the level of his agitation. To some extent this situation was repeated twice a day during those last four weeks. It took a considerable toll of my nervous system, and perhaps was partly why I had such a violent reaction to his death.

When things were normal – and normal is a relative term – when I was in communication with him, knew he understood me, I told him about my business, in which he took a great pride and interest, and in which, latterly, he had been involved, so that he could still feel he was part of our ordinary life. I showed him small things I had bought. It did occur to me that brass door-knockers were a rather unorthodox thing to take in on hospital visiting, but I did not care. I boasted about the takings; he need not worry about money. I told him some of the things we had done. I brought to his bed, second-hand, normal life; the camellia was coming out, we had washed the dogs, I had painted the garden furniture. Ordinary, mundane things; I was going to dinner with a girl friend; the many phone calls, who had rung, who had asked about him and sent their love. I told him he was a good-looking bugger and he responded with a very characteristic collective monosyllable. I told him he was getting better-looking every day, and he smiled and was pleased. And, like everything else, it was true; his skin was clear and elastic, and his hair, free from dressing, was as fine as a young child's.

*

When does someone die? What is dying? There may be medical, ethical and technical answers. But I know that one Thursday I visited Stanley in the morning, and when we looked at each other – and it was the same level look I had from my daughter minutes after she was born – I knew my clever, moody, difficult, charming and loved husband had left me. He was on an ice-floe, the current taking him slowly one way while I went another. And driving home along the motorway, I thought of the lines from Eliot's 'The Hollow Men':

This is the way the world ends,
Not with a bang but a whimper.

I just knew what was happening, just knew no power in heaven or earth could change this, could stop it.

So that was when he left. Although he lived for another three weeks, that was when I lost the 'ordinary' person. He had crossed a line, like Tom Tiddler's ground, and I could not follow.

*

The professional help and kindness were incalculable. Some of it was a mixed blessing. The social worker wanted to counsel me, but I was rather unpromising material. Many years before, Stanley and I had both, in our different ways, fought his alcoholism and the problems of sobriety. These problems really require a book of their own. Alcoholism is a complicated and incurable disease; it is a physical, mental and spiritual illness, regarded by the WHO as one of the great 'killing' diseases in the world. 'Just for today I will not have a drink' can build up into day upon day, and then into weeks and months and years, and ours added up to 22 years. But there is terrible emotional 'scar tissue'. Sobriety is considerably more complex than just not drinking.

I had already been through too much.

Perhaps no one outside the Fellowship (of Alcoholics Anonymous) will understand or be anything but shocked when I say how glad I was of that alcoholism, then and now.

I had, over twenty years before, looked death in the face, because had Stanley not attained sobriety then he would, quite certainly, have died within three to six months.

I knew, branch and root, what I felt, and because on this he and I were indivisible, I am perfectly sure that he too found a proved and tested framework and practical philosophy on which to fall back. Alcoholism is, after all, only one of the faces of death. It was natural to both Stanley and me – particularly in moments of stress and crisis – to take life a day at a time. Sometimes I, in the tumult of emotion, had to cut this down even further, to take half a day at a time; occasionally it had to be a few minutes at a time.

So, despite my tears to the social worker, I was calm inside. I did not think: 'How tragic he has to die so soon,' but was only glad he had lived so long. Being only human, I was so sad he would not live to see his daughter's children, but I was far happier that he had done the most important thing, had nineteen years of unalloyed joy in watching her grow to be a woman.

Through my training, my experience, my 'conditioning' at

18

the meetings, I had learned to share; to know my story was the same as the others, to listen, identify and learn from someone else, and to know they were the same as I am.

My husband's death was not secret and private, I spread the news and the feelings around. It was not so much impulse but a prompting from an agency I do not identify that made me use the telephone. I had a bill afterwards that was so large I thought it was a misprint, but had it been multiplied by ten, every penny was worth it.

One night I rang a man who had done work in the house, and he had become a friend. He told me how his crippled baby sister had died; her nightdress had caught fire while she was with a sitter and they were all out at a party. 'It destroyed us as a family,' he said, speaking as the eldest of four children. 'We none of us, ever, spoke about it.' I couldn't believe it. 'My brother is a hopeless neurotic, my sister has tremendous problems.' Perhaps my phone call helped him more than it helped me. Later, when Anne and I read 'The Sorrow Tree',* I quoted this to her, and we were glad of our own sorrow. Whatever else we felt, it was not self-pity.

The chaplain gave comfort when I was afraid. Logically, if you believe in God, you must acknowledge the Devil. Had I been born two hundred years ago, I should have had no problem, but I am the product of a tremulous twentieth century. I had to ask, 'Was it the whisky, was it the emotion?' But I do know that one night, black wings beat all round my head as I sat in my kitchen which is the heart of my home. My hands clenched, beating on the scarred table where I knead the bread, I shouted down the evil, 'You shan't have him! You shan't have him!'

Normality and morning light brought shyness, and it took courage to ring the chaplain. He at once agreed to meet me at the hospice. He took me seriously: 'The forces of evil are very powerful.' I did not feel embarrassed when he prayed for me.

*Traditional story from the Jewish Hasidic teaching.

He asked: 'Shall we go up and see your husband? Would he like to see me?' Beyond normal manners, I said, 'I shouldn't think so.' But gently and implacably, he controlled the situation. 'I'll just pop into the ward. I won't tire him.' He came out a few minutes later and said, 'I just held his hand and said a prayer, and he gave me such a charming smile.'

And the black, twisted sourness never came back to me again.

I lost all faith. I felt Stanley would go alone into an empty darkness. I had only two days – not forty – in the wilderness. But I had never before understood this bleakness. Stanley's time in hospital coincided with Easter, the time of death, the promise of rebirth. I had a new understanding of this great festival. I shall always be glad of this. And how Stanley, our lifelong atheist, would have laughed had he known that his death was a religious experience. I would have told him, because then there was nothing that was not worth saying, but by then he had gone beyond the higher subtleties and refinements of speech.

The professionals kept telling me I must start the mourning process now, in advance of death. Perhaps I misunderstood them, because I resisted. It seemed like wishing someone dead. There is such a universal fear that you may actually cause a death by wishing it. Perhaps the chaplain was trying to say 'Accept'. And this I did. From the moment the doctor talked to me, I never doubted his verdict. The previous weeks had conditioned me to knowing unconsciously; all the doctor did was to give authority to what I already knew.

The social worker said, 'Of course, your husband might recover. There are miraculous remissions . . .' I found this terribly distressing. I rushed from her office to the chaplain full of horror and guilt, because by then I had gone so far down my own particular road that had there been a miraculous remission I do not think I could have retraced my steps, accepted Stanley again.

20

It was spring. People say death is hard in the spring; I should have found snow, sleet, hard frost much more depressing. It was wonderful; warmth and new life, flowers, streaming sunshine in a golden wind.

For me, April was not the cruellest month.

*

Our daughter's birthday is in the middle of that month. Until the actual morning, I did not dare to write 'From Dad and Mum' on her card, on her presents. I told her they were truly from her father; I had talked to him about them, I had taken his money to buy her gifts. But I was so frightened that he might die on that very day; it would have been unbearably cruel.

A friend, with a trained scientific mind, surprised me: 'Stanley will die when he has finished his work here.' And he still had twelve more days of work to do.

*

When Stanley was first admitted to hospital, I said that when the tests were finished, he should come home. It would be natural and fitting; a woman should be married from her home, a man should die in his home. We live in a house which is a hundred and fifty years old. It must have witnessed much copulation, much birth and death in the days before the latter were all done tidily, invisibly, in hospitals.

We began to talk of nurses, bed downstairs, near a lavatory and washbasin. Then, within the first week, Stanley had two massive fits one night. Very late, a nurse telephoned to tell me he had broken his arm. It was rotten with cancer,

21

and because of the condition of his lungs and brain, an anaesthetic was impossible, so the arm was left, strung up in a sling.

The doctor agreed with my decision that I could not look after such a sick man at home, particularly with an unset break. Unhappily, this conversation was not reported to the sister, who was busy still making plans to send Stanley back home.

I had to fight through this distressing situation a second time. It still seems to me a dreadful thing to deny a man entry into his home, to reject him. I believe totally the decision was correct, but I still cannot reconcile it. And how I cried; ugly, ugly tears. I told the doctor, 'You are the only man I have ever known who is not embarrassed by a woman crying' – but I noticed he was pretty quick to leave the room, sending in a nurse with a cup of tea.

Afterwards, I asked a man why men should be so upset by crying when tears are such a relief. He said men feel they should be able to do something, they feel inadequate, helpless, frightened and ashamed by weeping. Perhaps they feel as I did, with the one fit I saw Stanley have, his face contorted as he fell from his bed, his arms and legs thumping convulsively on the floor; a violence for which there was no control, a helplessness while waiting for it to pass.

But, oh, the kindness of the staff; I see the snub-nosed nurse, and the sweet, worn face of the staff sister. In their busy rush with too many very sick men to look after, they all found time for me. When I cried, they said, 'You're coping very well,' and took me off to an office, gave me tissues and cups of tea. Soon, as a precaution, I pinched a couple of Stanley's big, sensible hankies and kept one in my pocket.

That was part of our pattern. I never expect to cry, and I always do. When our daughter was small, at nativity plays, school prize-giving, I would always suddenly sniff deeply, turn to Stanley and say, 'Lend me a hankie.' He would smile, give me a spare one and say, 'Why don't you ever think to bring your own?' At home, Anne would say, embarrassed

22

and indignant, 'I *heard* you, Mum!' and they would both tease me.

*

My greatest fear was that one day Stanley might not recognise me. I thought it was going to happen when he peered down an empty ward over my shoulder and said, 'What are those people doing? They look like spies, plotting something.' I turned, saw only bare polished boards in the sunshine, and realised it was a hallucination. I said, 'Just visitors. Quite harmless.'

One evening he looked at me down the bed, narrowed his eyes and said, 'Where is my wife?' Straight from the novels, I really did feel my scalp contract. I said, 'I'm here, I'm your wife.' 'Oh,' he replied. 'I know you. You're the woman I love, but did I ever marry you?'

A crumb from a lifetime, a feast for a lifetime.

*

Now that I can look back, I think we had no difficulty in talking, because all that was really necessary had been said. When we left the house to drive to the hospital, I knew he would never walk up the steps again. I carried his overnight case and he took my hand – such a rare gesture – and said, 'You know, we've had a good life together. It's all been worth while.' My words rushed up, spontaneous: 'It's been a bit rough at times, but that's all melted away now and all I can remember is how much I love you.'

So I drove him to hospital in tears, in truth.

*

I decided quickly it was better to anticipate the second unspoken question – what about the pain? Well, what about it? I don't know; it wasn't me doing the suffering. The doctor promised: 'We will control the pain and he will keep his dignity.' I think they succeeded. I watched very closely. At no time was Stanley contorted; his hands were relaxed, his feet still, his body and face calm.

Sometimes, he was tense and restless; irritable, angry and aggressive, but then that was a normal pattern. But when I felt he was unquiet, I went to the nurses and said I thought perhaps his pain levels had risen, they should increase the dosage. He could not ask, the words would not come; he was too proud and probably would not have asked himself. So, my job was to watch, to ask for him. And, blessedly, the sister said, 'We pay great attention to what you say. You are his wife, and you know him so much better than we do.' They acted when I asked, and I had no fear.

*

One day I realised I had requested an increased dosage twice within five days. I asked the sister what happened when we reached the safety level of the drugs.

And then there was perhaps my worst time for tears. I sat in her office, she held my hand, and I cried straight through half a new box of tissues she opened for me. And, wise woman that she is, she said I must take matters a day at a time, that I had seen how up and down my husband was, that she had plenty of safety margin in hand.

I had cups of tea, but I had to wait an hour before I was calm enough to drive home, had to take a longer route, following the guide and control of traffic lights because my judgment was so shaky I was not really safe to drive. I can see every detail of her office. She was obviously a dog lover. There were pictures of spaniels pinned up all round the walls, and a print of a Van Gogh picture, a street scene with a café and evening lights.

*

Then we moved to phase two, the last three weeks. Stanley left the hospital and, at my request, went to a local hospice. For a day, I had terrible cold feet, uncertainty and dread that I had made the wrong decision.

But within twenty-four hours I knew it was right, how lucky we were. The hospice was only five minutes' drive away; I could easily walk there if the car broke down. If Stanley was unwell, and he had pneumonia a couple of times because his ribs were too sore for him to cough properly to clear the matter from his lungs, then I could stay for just ten minutes, sit while he slept, feel he knew me. I did then what I used to do for my child when she was young and could not sleep. I stroked his head, told him poems, the AA prayers, recited that most ancient prayer 'Matthew, Mark, Luke and John, Bless the bed that I lie on.'* I had them, too, my versions of those four supporters, round my bed, round me, all the time, four particular friends whose strength and love never failed me; always one at the end of the telephone, just listening.

The hospice ward was spacious; calm and cool yet warm and airy. For the first day, Stanley was bewildered and terrified. He didn't understand, he didn't want to take his pills, and I knew he was afraid we were poisoning him. But he settled. And, oh, how good they were! He was always spotlessly clean; laundered sheets and fresh pyjamas every day. If he had a 'good' day, took all his food, the nurses were proud and excited. If he were tetchy and bad-tempered, they didn't mind. They let me take in his favourite tinned fruit, little treats.

*Known as 'The White Paternoster'.

The staff said, 'We're here to look after you as much as him.' They held me and helped me when the ache below my throat burst into tears as I turned the corner out of the ward.

Sometimes, he was so ill, I could only sit and hold his good hand, lay my other hand on his arm, trembling now with perpetual palsies. I felt as if the cancer beneath the skin was a golden dragon, rushing, triumphant, laughing at me. I could feel the tremble for hours afterwards. At home, nothing I could do would wash the tremor from my palm. Weeks later, I put my hand on the rail of an underground escalator and felt the soft throb of machinery, so reminiscent – and so utterly terrifying.

It all came together in a rush. A staff sister said, 'I think sometimes this is worse for the families,' but I said, 'No. I can walk out of here, into the sunshine, start the car, light a cigarette, drive away. He can't. He's stuck with it.' I knew, whatever had happened in the last weeks, we had been playing games. When I went to see him, he kissed me, his lips moving against my cheek in the familiar way. I could hold his hand; it was warm and strong. One day, soon, neither of these things would happen. That was what it was all about.

One sister said, when I commented on the strength of his grip, 'When I was doing his sling this morning, he got hold of me and, really, if we weren't in hospital, I don't know what people would have thought!' I laughed, longed to tell him, to tease him.

I knew then I had begun the long road of not sharing any more, ever again.

And so I learned what it was all going to be about for me. I would never, ever again in my life, use family shorthand; say a word, a phrase, that by association hammered out through years of living together, conveys a whole host of meanings that need no further explanation.

*

I saw three pictures in my mind during those hospice days. Myself, rushing headlong down a black helter-skelter; it all happened so quickly. And the land at the bottom was flat, dried and with black, burnt trees. I saw Stanley, a range of mountains with all the softening vegetation gradually stripped away; pointed and jagged rock against a skyline, essentials. I saw myself, too; a small ravine through which a torrent of water and emotion and knowledge had poured, cutting back the soft bank in layers, deepening it to the bedrock foundations.

I knew I should never again bother with trifles and this would make many future relationships uncomfortable.

I found Stanley's death was like an emotional sieve, shaking a great riddle, showing people as they truly are, separating the dross from the nuggets, and the nuggets shone, clear and pale, fine gold.

There was one member of his family, with whom we had always been on normal, friendly terms. From the moment Stanley went into hospital, she never rang. When he died, she never contacted me, never wrote, didn't come to his funeral, has never spoken to me since. It was not easy for me to follow friends' advice: 'Put it behind you, don't mind, don't bother, it's not worth it.' For a long, long time the hurt and bewilderment kept coming and knocking at the door of my heart.

There was an old friend, bringing up her young child alone on a small salary. When she got my letter, she rang from Australia, and I heard her voice for the first time in nineteen years: 'I just wanted you to know that we love you.'

So, I learned to know people, one from the other.

Undiluted truth is very strong meat for anyone's stomach. I had made a qualitative leap into a new dimension when I heard it from the doctor. But it is not for everyday living.

*

27

And then it happened.

Anne and I were both going to visit at lunch time, but the hospice rang, sending for us. Stanley was now in a side ward. His eyelids flickered when I kissed him. I held his hand, and also Anne's. We were together, linked, just once more; a small, united family who had always liked each other so much.

I left him alone with his youngest child, his only daughter; so adored and loved, with no marring of the relationship in nineteen years. He had adored her from the moment she was born, in the delivery room saying, 'Isn't she lovely?' – the first of countless times I was to hear that phrase!

She said later that she felt someone stand beside her at the bed, turned, looked through the inner window and saw, with surprise, that I was still in the corridor.

I went into the room and she left us both, ran in tears to the car. Alone, I did what I used to do for the young child when troubled, before sleep, on leaving home, made with my right thumb the sign of the cross on his forehead, and I said the words I had known for the past six weeks I would say: 'They'll all be waiting for you; Big Alex, Archie, your Mum. Certainly, my Auntie Joane, she couldn't be left out!' I looked over my shoulder, thinking a nurse stood there. But it was only a tremendous concentration of smiling, loving kindliness.

And so I knew he was being fetched. It was time for me to go.

Anne and I drove home, and the hospice rang twenty minutes later to say that he had died.

And we were so happy. Not because it was a 'release'. Just joy and laughter and tranquillity.

*

It was that first evening that I learned that death is unimportant, makes no difference at all.

28

After supper, my daughter called me, serious and alarming. 'Mum, I must talk to you.' She was standing in the middle of the kitchen floor, holding something wrapped in brown paper. 'Ages ago, when I was quite small, when we moved here . . .' 'You were about eleven?' 'Yes. Dad gave me this, and he said I was to put it away and give it to you on the night that he died.'

She had kept the promise, faithful to the last. Newly framed in the past few days was his photograph. It is a dreadful photo; he looks like a shady second-hand car salesman. I have put it away. But that one gesture, so utterly typical, brings Stanley back, recalls a thousand incidents more vividly than anything else could possibly have done; the clear elusiveness of a dream the next morning. And with that gift came great anger that he should have put such a weight, a responsibility, on a young child. I was so angry that had he not been dead, I could have killed him. I was as angry as I had ever been with him in life.

Death made absolutely no difference at all.

Much later that night, when my daughter had gone to bed, the dogs lay in their baskets in the kitchen, as I sat with yet another whisky, I found truth at the bottom of the glass. I was now available. No longer could I say, 'My husband will speak to you,' 'I must talk to my husband.' That night I realised I had stepped back, out of the marriage state. I was a fish that had been thrown back into the river. I was sexually available.

And that is how I went to bed, to begin my grieving.

*

Grief comes to all of us; sometimes it is gentle, a long, soft 'minding'. For me, it was devastating; I instantly knew a desolation I had not previously guessed existed.

In our stormy, contentious life, vital and active, I had

29

never realised how deep was our relationship. I felt like a tree, split by lightning, roots exposed.

Nothing was lost; no word, no thought, no emotion. I went back to what a friend termed 'the hand-in-hand days', and they were all suddenly there, intact, total recall; old jealousies and angers; desperate joy, minute tendernesses, all growing quick, deep tendrils that had rushed underground, secretly turned into vast tough roots. In the bread-and-butter roughage of daily life, I had been quite unaware of this. I was swamped by pain, yet surprised and amazed by it.

*

Grief means the same for everyone: loss; never more; having to adjust and accept the fact that something rare and precious has gone for ever.

I realised that for over half my lifetime, there was no hurt or worry that had not been made better when I shared it. There had been no joy or triumph that had full meaning, been really savoured until I had rushed home: 'I'm a genius!' and watched the quiet, amused smile that seemed to make his very spectacles glint with wry pleasure. He was my 'friend of the mind', my 'talking friend'. I shall not find his like again.

The day after the funeral, an elderly friend met me in the road and said, 'Thank you for a lovely party yesterday. I did enjoy myself!' It was an unorthodox tribute, and how I longed for a hot-line to heaven, to ring up and tell Stanley, who would have laughed himself silly. I longed, too, to tell him other things: of his son, so clever and so vague. I had asked him to take charge of the collection at church, and he had wandered back to the house after the service, leaving all the cash behind, unattended, in the porch.

The hospital padre told me of an old lady who had kept her

living room untouched, always said to the empty armchair, 'Good-night, my dear.' I said, 'I wouldn't do that. It's not healthy.' I am not so arrogant now. I know better.

*

People wondered if it was difficult to come back to the house, but it never once was. At some moment when Stanley was in hospital, the house changed, felt different when I opened the front door. It was as if, with typical sensitive courtesy, Stanley had deliberately withdrawn himself from it, left us free to be peaceful in our sanctuary.

For a few weeks, everything had been left exactly as it was when we closed the front door together, walked down the steps for the last time; the table I had put by his chair, the rug for his knees, his books, scraps of paper, a pencil stub and unexplained paper-clips. Then one day, gently, I began to tidy everything away; no feeling of disloyalty, of destroying him, just a natural slipping into a new pattern.

I was not troubled to sleep alone, nor bothered by the empty bed. After a time, I stripped it, put a cover over it. A single bed in a high, airy room would look out of proportion. I have just left it.

The dogs, however, presented us with problems of their own. When Stanley first went into hospital, they pined. They lay about in corners, ears down, tails hanging. There was none of the usual joyful excitement when we went for walks. Perhaps they were sensitive to the abnormal atmosphere and mood in the house, but they moped, were not their usual selves. One dog was unwell, and when I took him to the vet I said, 'My husband has just died. This dog is so unhappy, I'm sure he's pining.' The vet looked at me: 'There's nothing you can do. He'll just have to work through it.' 'Just like us?' His eyes smiled: 'Exactly.'

One night, just after Stanley died, all the dogs became

violently disquieted. They woke Anne and me up, running round, barking, whining and scratching, and there was no way we could soothe them for well over an hour. I held them, feeling their hard little bodies tremble. They had never behaved like this before, nor have they done so since. I could not but wonder; did his spirit come back to visit?

*

Turning out the clothes was hard; a horrible job. I have necessarily done it several times before in the family, and each time I swore it would be the last. But yet again I had to do it. It was my responsibility; there was no one else. I just had to take a deep breath, and removed armfuls to the nearest charity shop. I think I should have felt disloyal, as if I were rapidly expunging Stanley, had he not been a man who placed no value at all, had no interest, in material possessions. For the children, there was no personal memento, because he had nothing, except his watch for his eldest son.

I remember talking recently of future hopes and plans for the business and he just asked, quietly, 'Why?' 'For the sake of it, to prove I can do it. It has to be measured in money, there's no other yardstick, but for the inner satisfaction.' He smiled, it passed, it was acceptable, the motive was pure.

The papers were worse, much worse. Inevitably, I found scraps, notes and letters I should never have read. I found a copy of a letter to his previous wife, written before our marriage. I knew of its existence at the time it was written, but it was not a happy thing to find then, within weeks of Stanley's death. The letter brought the unhappy past back to the present, or took the present back to the past. Nothing was lost; the old antagonisms just sleeping. It was the unacceptable face of the unity of life and death. I had forgotten, or overlooked, that some secret flowers have stinging leaves.

32

I tried to say, 'It doesn't matter, it's all over and done with,' but it wasn't true. It was a great battle to force myself to realise it was just something Stanley had filed away once, simply forgotten, that he would never, otherwise, have left me to find something so distressing.

I fell into an elephant-trap for the heart, and pulled myself out: 'We've had a good life together . . .'

I found one or two things that, by their lonely courage, were very moving; things a writer by trade had written privately for himself. I took his bravery and have tried to make it my own. Some letters and documents brought back the ancient battle – storms and heartache, tears at midnight – now utterly meaningless, cobwebs or dried leaves in a forgotten corner. What time spent and energy wasted. We were idiots, baying at a false moon; we did not get our priorities right. Sometimes, now, when I see other couples in contention and at odds with each other, I want to shake them and say, 'Don't waste time, love each other as hard as you can, while you can.'

I found the pathetic detritus everyone collects, little things like book matches from a restaurant and mementoes from occasions I had not realised had meant so much to him. And I felt as if I had failed him, and also that I was prying. In all our life together, I always asked permission to take something from his pockets, as he always asked mine to look in my handbag. We always paid each other for postage stamps. I cried and cried.

All these things were what a friend was to call later, in his own grief, 'little booby-traps for the heart'.

*

I knew music would be a problem. There is no protection against familiar melodies. Probably all my life I shall suddenly overhear one of 'his' songs, and with the evocation

33

will come the tears. To immunise myself as much as possible, I played all his favourite records, over and over and over, and in the end found his taste in jazz and blues music as uninteresting to me as it has always been.

*

I had to accept there would be this sudden nostalgia, bringing with it pain. Months after Stanley died, I had to take my daughter to the dental hospital. And I remember how we had all gone there together, when Anne was small, how comforting and understanding he had been when we were both just anxiously worried parents. While Anne was with the consultant, I wept and wept in the high and marbled hall where the bronze busts gaze sightlessly at each other, and I saw Stanley so clearly, missed him so desperately. An aimlessly wandering patient looked at me, very startled, and I knew how Stanley would laugh to know he had been mourned so fiercely in such an extremely unlikely place.

*

All parting is a little death. Lovers returning home from the station farewell will think of a dozen things they meant to say, a dozen things they want to share. They can run to the telephone, write a letter. Friends can save up the little significant things they noticed, felt, heard, saw, until they next meet. But death is final: no more sharing. Ever.

The trouble was, I went on noticing and listening and seeing, just as I did when we were away from each other, and I could take them home; little anecdotes and scraps of information from mutual friends that over cups of coffee and drinks I would spill out higgledy-piggledy, knowing Stanley would laugh, be interested – or bored – and I didn't have to care. And I couldn't stop collecting things for him, but I have no one to give them to.

I found I simply had the habit of loving, and death made no difference at all. The machinery spun on, free-wheeling, even though the motor had stopped.

*

Families, other complete families, are a major pain, a weal across the hand, no evasion.

Driving to the hospice one day, Anne and I passed some friends; parents and one child. They were doing nothing more exciting than washing their car, and all three returned our wave. Separately, both Anne and I hated them; fierce, deep, primitive resentment. With much difficulty, Anne and I talked about it together, lanced the poison and accepted the reality. They were still a family, and we never would be again. Once more – and the time that seemed so endless now seems so short – I am again an outsider, I have joined a sub-section of society.

*

It is such a simple thing, to be a family; millions and millions of families, in all shapes and sizes. For us, we were three people of independent, irritable intelligence, who lived together and liked each other. We had our own words, our in-house jokes and catch-phrases. We led separate, busy lives, but each evening we ate at the kitchen table, shared the tiny events of the day, laughed at each other and at the antics of humanity and closed ranks against outsiders.

Family life is such an ordinary thing, enjoyed and, perhaps

rightly, not valued at the time but simply accepted like air and good health that you only notice when you no longer have it. We had adapted and moulded to each other; the bliss of sagging elastic, the comfort of heel-trodden slippers.

Now that I am alone and solitary, I observe with a keener eye, a sharper understanding. Because of my own experience, I can hold up an infallible litmus paper to the quality of happiness in other families – and enjoy it; the idiom may be different, the experience is my own. I do not resent death, which has taken away my happiness. I am only glad to know that I have had that happiness and fulfilment, because not everyone does.

Luckily, I never had the alarming anger that comes to many in grief. I never felt, 'How dare you leave me? By dying, you have caused me so much pain.' I know many people do feel this – my own mother did, and highly alarming she was, too – and are bewildered and ashamed by it. I have fairly high levels of aggression, so I do not know how I escaped this syndrome, but I was thankful. All I felt was a new impatience with trivia and inessentials, with people who had hurt me. I spoke my mind, very clearly and in terms I do not normally use. Not surprisingly, that caused some surprise and affront. Today, I wonder if I was as immune from this 'anger' as I had imagined at the time. Then, I just knew that to harbour resentments was a luxury I could not afford. It was too dangerous. I did not have much balance, nor any longer a partner to help me regain a sense of perspective to deal with the aggressions.

*

And the dreams. You cannot guard yourself against them, and the bad dreams that make you afraid to go to sleep the next night are the worst of all. I had one nightmare about Stanley that was so utterly horrific that at three in the morning I had to wake Anne, and ask her to make me some tea. None of the few subsequent dreams has been happy; always Stanley was in a crowd, walking away from me.

But I am not afraid. For the three months before Stanley went into hospital, I woke every morning and had to reach down deep inside myself for a ration of courage for that day. When he was admitted to hospital, I had to keep on finding courage, then a diffident kind. I do not think a dream would confound me, because I had to practise my courage and, like a muscle, it has grown stronger with that use.

*

His children gave me special problems. They are all grown-up, but no one is really an adult until a parent has died. That death means everyone changes places, has moved one up in the family scale, becomes an older generation, if not The Older Generation.

One evening, to my daughter and one of the boys, I said: 'We are all going to say goodbye to Dad, very soon.' They looked at me, amazed, and I went on: 'But that is what this means. We shall all say goodbye at different times and in different ways. I expect, because I am his wife, I shall be the last to say goodbye, but it may be too ugly in the end, perhaps I shan't be able to take it. I hope not, but there is no point in pretending you are going to be brave when you haven't been tested. We don't know what is going to happen to him or to any of us in the next week or two. And his death will be something different to each of us. We should begin, now, to think what his death will mean.'

Much later that night, my daughter came down to the kitchen in her nightie: 'Dad will never see the man I marry.' I nodded: 'No, he won't. He always hoped he'd live to see you have your babies, but he won't now. But when you have your own children, one day Dad will look up at you from your

37

child's face; just occasionally, my father smiles up at me from yours.'

One boy, after his father's death, said, 'Companionship. I've got sons of my own, I haven't seen all that much of Dad in the last few years, but he was always a companion, someone I could talk to, even if we didn't say much.' How I wished Stanley, so diffident in his relationships, so insecure in love, could have heard that.

Perhaps I, too, sing the same song, only the words are different.

*

All I have written is only a repetition of what I found in the small body of writing upon grief I have discovered. Different facets, often a similar idiom; sometimes a tiny, vital phrase, so you know you are not alone, others have felt this too; comfort in the chartless maze into which you are thrown by early, violent grief.

I wonder how I could bring myself to write this, not only because all writing is difficult – the terror of the white page – but to know what to say.

Early on, I went off and made notes, because I knew that such intense emotions would pass and be readily forgotten. I was so ashamed of myself for doing this that, almost superstitiously, I made all the notes outside my home. I then put them in such a safe place that when I did begin to write, I could not find them, and it was not until I had almost finished that I discovered the folder. I went on writing, and then referred to the notes, and there was nothing I had forgotten, and I had no need of them after all. Everything that was important had gone straight down, printed in black and white, as if typeface had bitten into a stencil skin in my mind.

It has been difficult to write, too, because I was brought up not to use the word 'I' when writing. To use the third person seemed to me to make everything I wanted to say heavy and pretentious. I had to accept that I was showing myself without my skin, and therefore to write in the first person is the only possible way, even if it opens me to a charge of egotism.

And writing this has been the hardest work I have ever done; not just the physical reluctance all writers know to take up the pen, to sit at the typewriter. It was hard to look back on such personal pain, to relive it, to expunge it and, in doing so, fear that the memory would be lost forever. I seemed to hug the grief, prodded at it, tried to keep the pain alive as if that pain was something tangible, something I wanted to hold on to, a last link, a last memento.

*

Shortly after my husband's death, I went to stay briefly with an old family friend in Spain. Everyone agreed it would be a good thing for me, a change, a rest. What we had all overlooked was that I had totally and completely lost my self-confidence, and the simple flight I made alone was one of the most terrifying things I have ever done.

Because, without question, my hostess and I both loved Stanley in our different ways, we could talk honestly and without disloyalty about his bad points; how moody, how difficult, at times, too, how cruel he could be. It rounded out the memory; helped the past person and the present person in my mind to come together. Because the love and affection were there, it was not a case of speaking ill of the dead. The dead are gone; they do not care. To speak ill is a terrible thing for the living, those who are left, because the person is not here to refute the charges, to give balance, to remind you of their good points. Few people are saints; it is dishonest to deify; very hard, and certainly for me, very necessary, to strike that balance.

39

So, the talk was good; the conversations helpful. But more than anything else I shall remember Soledad.

She was an elderly Spanish woman; streaked black hair, and rusty black clothes. She ran a tiny bar, wedged between an outcrop of rock and a cement football court and hedged by corrugated iron and beer crates. She was told – speaking no English – that my husband had just died. She seized my hands and to my astonishment and embarrassment, began to cry. She rocked backwards and forwards, archetypal grieving woman. Through the torrent of words I caught 'Jorge', and realised she was not so much sharing my grief as expressing her own. I recognised yet again that it always happens that way! The 'comforters' who came to see me – and I honoured their sincerity – were all of a pattern. They came still to tell their own tale, not to listen.

I asked when Jorge had died; seven years ago, and he was a 'good man', 'much man'. I was appalled; so much grief? For so long? For longer? For ever?

Soledad wept openly, unashamed. We are hedged about with inhibitions and are embarrassed by death, frightened by raw emotions. Anne and I found that it was we who had to comfort a local family, put them at ease. They did not fail us in kindness, love or concern, but they simply did not know what to say to us.

It was one of the saddest things. Grief put up a barrier, made loneliness lonelier.

I could feel that people were nervous that I would cry, create a scene. Death took me back to the birth of my daughter, who was tiny and frail and caused much concern. All new mothers, their emotions well and truly stirred, are very volatile, and I was also frantic with anxiety. The doctors then kept me at an emotional arm's length, rightly fearing I might erupt, and so it was with death.

*

After a little while, I found I could not talk to the children; they could not say what their father's death meant, how much they missed him, if at all. If they had not all been so good at visiting, so concerned, I might easily have thought they did not care, but I know that is not true. Even with our daughter, I felt she flinched if I mentioned his name. I said, 'This makes you feel awkward' – she was uneasy if I remarked, 'Wouldn't Dad have been pleased about that?'

*

All my close friends contributed something; a word, a remark, a tiny gesture of loving concern. One came with a huge bunch of cowslips from her country garden, and a funny story about her eccentric sister. Her gift was laughter, and what greater gift can anyone ever bring? I shall feel a debt to her for ever, because the hard, tight strain left Anne's face and she looked again what she was, a pretty nineteen-year-old, her face relaxed and alight.

But in those first few months, the only really meaningful conversation I had was with a stranger, a neighbour, whose husband had died a few weeks after Stanley. By a great act of courage, I knocked on her door one afternoon, said I would go in for ten minutes, left two hours later.

We compared notes, and cried without noticing it, and it was such a help. It was such a relief to find what I was feeling was not unique. I had never really supposed that it was. But almost no one I normally met had shared the experience, so couldn't understand, or if they did, they couldn't talk about it.

*

One danger I found quickly, and still find, is to keep integrity, to remember as well and as honestly as I can, the person who was. It is so easy to put words into an absent mouth. It is very hard to be absolutely sure. To quote is a double-edged, fairy sword of great danger and potency.

*

Our contemporary society is frightened and embarrassed by death. It is a pity that many of the old customs of mourning should have been discarded.

Our robust Victorian ancestors were much more sensible and realised the practical value of formal mourning. It is a protection, an outward sign of the temporary, but disintegrating, process going on inside; a valid, visible reason that you may be excused from the problems and demands of life.

Today, we struggle on as if nothing had happened; bills, workmen, often a demanding job, all have to be coped with. There is no public allowance for, or understanding of, that first dreadful phase; such total exhaustion that I often took half an hour before I could walk across the kitchen and make a cup of tea; short memory loss, so that things people said simply skated across my mind, leaving no mark. I had no concentration; forms were meaningless, I could neither read nor do a crossword.

*

After my husband died, I found I met many of the emotions I had experienced just after my daughter was born. I had a feeling of walking back to meet myself again. I could not drive very far. I felt shaky. I had a mild, passing attack of agoraphobia. I needed to be quiet, near home. I felt oddly detached; decisions were for other people.

I found life and death was a circle, a unit.

*

I look back.

I look back over nine months, to a time when life was still ordinary, coming events were only a flicker of marsh fire.

I went out one autumn evening into the garden and cut the dead-heads from the hollyhocks. As dusk fell, I slipped out of the house, across the road, to a patch of grass bordering a housing estate. There, in soft earth against a wall, I planted the seed-heads, pushing them down, smoothing them over.

I did not know why I did this, nor did I wonder at it.

I then came home, cooked dinner.

I never told a soul what I had done.

The green lies a hundred yards from my home. I did not walk over the grass until after Stanley's death. There, shouting scarlet and triumphant in the sun were the grown flowers. I was transfixed with an amazed ecstasy of joy. Then I knew that I should recover, would emerge from the black despair, would one day again become a whole person.

*

I abominate the phrase 'one parent family', and although it is now true of myself, I resent the label, that I am another statistic. All that has happened is, either by death or some matter of agreement, one parent is absent. That absence shows up most vitally in the lack of one parental duty; to provide a refuge to the child from the other parent's anger, be that anger only a snapping irritation and the refuge a secret sweet given privately.

A few nights after Stanley's death, my daughter irritated me; the universal, maternal litany: 'inconsiderate', 'thoughtless', 'unhelpful'. I was unreasonable, on edge – but so was she. I bit back the words, because if I upset her by a quick and thoughtless anger there was no one to say quietly, afterwards, 'Don't mind, don't pay any attention, Mum's tired, she didn't mean it.'

Death therefore means that I am no longer quite normal, I am changed. I have to make all the decisions, to try to be wise for two when I have no confidence that I could even be wise for myself.

I was so cross and bemused, because I had always seen myself as an independent adult, and here was the 'little girl' syndrome appearing. I wondered if I had been much less grown-up than I had supposed, if everything I had previously assumed was wrong and if I had in reality leaned on Stanley and been a clinging vine. I felt muddled and lost and unhappy; I had lost myself.

And yet if I had not relied on him, he would have felt rejected. For thirty years I had become close to someone, and his death was like a fast lorry crashing into a cul-de-sac. A lifetime's energy that had travelled one way, suddenly telescoped into reverse.

I compared myself unfavourably with spinster friends, who presumably have to cope alone with all the things I found so dauntingly difficult. Perhaps I am being kind to myself when I feel it is easier for them. They have evolved a life, a 'carapace', suited to one person, but I was left with all the structure of life for a family. We live in a house which was big for the three of us, large for two and is now enormous for one. Everything that family life entailed had a momentum and life of its own, and it was too big for me.

It is really only the passage of time that has helped. I find I have made decisions which are not too disastrously wrong, that I have battled with income tax and builders, and this has given me some confidence and self-respect. But all this has changed me; I am much tougher than I was.

44

I notice that Anne is protective, sometimes, in matters where her father took care of me. I am touched, but I know it should not happen. We manage, but we are different from other families; we are injured, maimed, and there is nothing anyone can do about it.

*

I was afraid – and still am afraid – because there is no one to protect me, particularly from myself, from sudden rash impulses and enthusiasms. Some fundamental change has occurred; I have become cautious, careful of myself. I have lost the luxury of spontaneity. I have to try to look deep into myself when seized by an idea, to assess, to ask my memories: 'What would you say?' I often – usually – disagreed with Stanley and fought for my own way. I miss the battles! I miss the judgment, the wisdom, the balance, the sense, the other view.

*

Those first weeks were such a time for high emotion, it was easy to forget that, by its very nature, death has enormous practical effects. I often automatically laid a third place at the table. And shopping was difficult. With only two of us living at home, I was in a fever of indecision; a pound of mince was too much, half a pound not enough. In the end, I bought a larger quantity, put a second meal in the freezer. It was difficult to adjust.

*

Because of their very intensity, I knew many of the emotions would pass, change, probably disappear. But there was one that persisted; elusive, difficult to put into words, still haunting. Perhaps it is fear, a near recognition of my own, of everyone's, mortality. It seemed dreadful that, ignorant and carefree, we had gone on holiday, sat in the sun on the cliff tops reading our books on a sheltered seat, and a year later Stanley was dead.

I felt, obscurely, that I should have known, that I should have been able to do something, that somehow I could have prevented his death. I know perfectly well that these feelings are beyond reason; that, of course, is the trouble with feelings! When I am tired – and in the early days I had to take great care of myself and not get tired, because when I was tired I was miserable – and depressed, these emotions seep out round the corners of the pressure of everyday life. I feel as if Fate had crept up on us unaware, and I am profoundly afraid.

I do not feel any guilt at the laughter and enjoyment since Stanley died, only of the careless laughter before. I have compared notes, and I know other people have felt many of my emotions, we share the same feelings. But this haunting guilt I cannot yet talk about, nor come to terms with.

*

The loss of my husband was inconvenient and expensive. I never realised until he had gone just how many small jobs he did around the house. A toilet-roll holder that has pulled loose from the wall, Stanley would have plugged and reset. Now, I either have to try to do it myself, or find a handyman and pay him. Sometimes, there are two or three trivial chores I cannot do myself, and they snowball together into a major, daunting problem.

I have learned to change electric plugs, and with a sense of wild, excited achievement. Perhaps I shall learn other things.

Friends kept saying, 'Do let us know if there is anything we can do . . .' But much seems so petty, and I am too shy or too proud to bother them.

*

The church was comforting and helpful. Everyone connected locally was kind, practical, matter-of-fact and practised. The new vicar was co-operative over the rather unorthodox service. As we planned it, he said, 'Your husband sounds such an interesting man. I wish I had met him, I think I should have liked him so much.'

He said as much, in the service; his sincerity touched everyone and was commented upon.

My own rather haphazard approach to religion fluctuated wildly. For months, I cried so much I could not sit through a service. Sometimes I found going to church comfortable, sometimes unbearable. As the wilder excess of grief passed, so did this, and was replaced by a calmer balance.

*

I suppose the sixty-four-thousand-dollar question is, 'Would I like Stanley back? Now?' Sitting alone in a pub recently, waiting for friends, I wondered and found to my surprise the answer was 'no'. I think now Stanley was iller for much longer than we had realised, and that accounted for his erratic behaviour, his irritability, his hectoring crossness. Because I did not then understand, I was intolerant; hurt and angry, I went away inside myself, alone.

One night he said, 'Don't leave me, even if I drive you away,' and I replied, 'No. I'm one of the ones that stay.' But

47

it has taken me months to get behind those last years, to distil his essence, and if having him back implied going back to those times, those recent difficult days, then, 'no'.

There is a relief in being alone. It is lovely to cook all the food I like and which he, our pernickety eater, hated. And as I sat in the bar, looking at the warm lights reflected in the copper top, I thought of all the times we had sat together, peacefully, in his drinking days, before the bad times, when it was still fun, and realised I would not have him back because he had not gone. His essence I carry within me all the time. Often I cannot feel it, but I know it; it is still there.

We were two intelligent, independent, proud, strong-willed people, often at odds with each other, but who occasionally found perfect contentment together. And these times made all the rest worth while. I very often mentally packed my suitcase, but I never went. Fundamentally, I didn't want to.

*

I keep saying, 'There is no death.' This is nonsense. Of course, there is death. But death, the death of my husband, was not what I had expected or imagined, although since I had never really thought about it before, I cannot say exactly what I had expected.

What I do know now is that death is not an end. A change, yes; immense and profound, but not an end.

There is a subtle but very deep social change, and since humans are social animals, this is immensely important. It cannot be discounted and considered trivial in the matter of grieving. My whole status in society has changed dramatically; my label, my external and my internal pictures of myself are utterly different.

When I was young and first married, I became a young wife. Then I became a divorcee, slightly shocking not so long ago. Then I remarried and became a married woman and respectable. I remember the rather militant feminist daughter of a friend being so shocked as she watched me fill in a passport application form and me putting my occupation as 'Married Woman'. 'But you are all sorts of other things!' she exclaimed, 'I'd rather die than put that!' But that was what I was. I liked being a married woman, a housewife. I liked saying 'we'; I enjoyed being collective. I hadn't liked being solitary; I knew it too well. And having enjoyed being collective, I was sad that, after what seemed such a short time, I was again alone.

I had a child, became a mother and sometimes lost my own identity and simply became 'Anne's Mum'. Like most women, I played a number of different and sometimes overlapping roles.

And then I became a widow.

The change was as profound as the others, but with one major difference. The other status changes had been with my consent and co-operation. But nobody had asked me if I wanted to become a widow; it was forced on me. I was outraged.

When you become a widow, you have a label, a tag. Very nicely, one is explained – I have done it myself – 'She's a widow.' Nobody ever bothers, on introduction, to say, 'She's a married woman,' or 'She's a spinster.'

I found I was excluded from the freemasonry of women. Friends who love their husbands deeply are not immune from complaining. We all understand this, but suddenly I found there were things they would not say because I no longer had a husband. It did not diminish our affection, but it set a limit to our conversation. I was afraid for a time I was always now going to be on the outside, until one woman friend – probably unconsciously – paid me a vast compliment by exploding with anger at something her husband had done. I was able to respond, and I was accepted back, part of 'the gang'.

Widowhood makes your friendships shift. A friend – and

there is much true affection between us – said, speculatively, 'You're very young to be a widow.' But I knew at once what she really meant: watch out, my husband is my husband and you're free!

Luckily, I do not live in circles where I go to formal dinner parties, where numbers matter. If I did so, now I should be a problem; an extra man would have to be asked, and in middle-aged circles people have settled as couples, spare men are difficult to find. Widows get left out.

I found out that society has its own built-in time-scale. After about six months, people's attitude changed; you are expected to have got over the death, whether or not you have.

I thought of all the depressing widow-women in literature. I did not see myself as a widow in the back street, nor a pathetic figure such as the one in John Masefield's poem. Nor did I care to think I might be referred to as 'the widow with her daughter'. Years ago, I was told about the champagne widow, and why Clicquot is known as 'The Widow'. I always hated the idea that 'widow' should be a title and turned into a proper name, as if widowhood were a profession.

And yet all this implies that collectively society acknowledges that the process of widowhood is very traumatic, and possibly-permanent. Even in these liberal and more 'enlightened' days, widows are in a very difficult position. Wives know you are free, men think you are available, society thinks in terms of 'good works'. I found personally – and I was irritated to find this – that when meeting strangers I had to explain, 'I am a widow.' My daughter is legitimate; I am not divorced. Why should I bother to explain? But I did!

*

A man came to do some work in the house. I felt unprotected

and that it would be rash to tell him, but could not help doing so: 'My husband has just died.' He gave me a long, assessing look from his blue eyes, wise with the sad wisdom of his ancient, oppressed race. 'I've had my sorrows, too. They mark you.'

*

Widowhood gave me a strange, and sad, knowledge too. Perhaps I was most conscious of this because almost none of my contemporaries are widowed. I have discussed this with one or two people, and we have agreed that there is no 'right time' for someone to be bereaved. If you are twenty-five, forty-five or seventy-five, whether the illness has been long or, as for us, swift and dramatic, there are the same problems in a different guise.

Anne and I both read, and re-read, the story of the Tree of Sorrows, where traditionally at the gate of heaven each traveller is allowed to hang his sorrows on the branches if he will pick up another person's burden from the tree. As they walk round, each person always returns and picks up his own again. Every time we argued with life, we realised this story was true!

Widowhood set me apart from my friends. I found it was like giving birth: I had to experience it before I knew what it felt like, and how I would behave at the time. I was apprehensive before my daughter was born: would I scream for hours in the manner so faithfully portrayed by early novelists? Until he comes under fire, no soldier knows if he is brave, can stand his ground before fear and pain, or if he will flinch and turn away. When faced by the extremes of birth and death, the best I could hope was that I did not need to be ashamed of myself.

Recently, I felt isolated with particularly close friends. They are much older than I, and they were talking, as we all talk, about the family and money. One used the phrase, 'Depends which of us goes first,' with that casual, academic air we all use. I felt my throat contract. Stanley and I used to say this, particularly when planning family finance. But now we know which of us went first, and in the end there wasn't time, and our plans came to nothing.

People said, 'I'm so sorry to hear you've lost your husband,' but what no one seemed to realise was that I had lost myself. And that was much more serious.

*

I keep looking back, not because I want to do so, nor to relive the good times. I find the past my only relevance; I go back to the 'me' that was to become 'I', when I was about eighteen.

I had to try to find my base, my fundamentals, because otherwise I could not build. Perhaps I had never lost this basis, but I felt that I had. For so long I had been less than myself because I was part of another person. In the end that has proved to be the most rewarding thing that can ever possibly happen, because while battering my ego it stretched the heart, but when the second person was wrenched away, I was lost. The internal machinery hummed, but the cog-wheels didn't connect, and I was helpless.

I cannot look forward, because there is nothing yet I want, so there is nothing to anticipate. Although I do not feel suicidal, I do sometimes feel, at bottom, the only thing I look forward to is death, when I shall see him and talk to him again. Yet, I enjoy life; rain, cold in my face; sun, warming my back; watching a puppy 'kill' his slipper; birds taking a dust bath.

I have – most luckily – just enough money. I could do more or less anything, go anywhere. There is nothing I positively want to do. I feel like a great ship, powerful sails set and full of strong wind, and with no hand at the helm, no course charted. I am frightened.

I very badly wanted a man – not in the usually debased sense of this phrase. I wanted a strong, male presence. Something deep inside me, something that makes me feminine, makes me woman, needed masculinity, a mirror in which I could reflect and so find myself. Without this I was formless, nothing. It was not that I needed he-man to take care of me; kind friends and sensitive professionals were ready to read forms, help me fill them in, look after everything. A part of me, so basic I had never discovered it before, needed masculinity so that I could re-mould my shape against it. I did not find what I needed, and I have never lost totally the feeling that I am a little 'skew-whiff', out of shape.

I sit still, in my home, my routine, my changed life, and wait. I wait for this phase to pass, and hope it will do so.

*

I have tried to keep as much in my life the same as was possible; the routine, the house, familiar. I have no alternative. I do the same things; empty the ashtray first thing, take downstairs my milk glass, cup and hot-water bottle in the morning. I look at the furniture we bought together; it is all meaningless. It belongs to a time when we were positive, active, starting, building. This, now, is limbo, aimless steps in the cactus land.

*

There is no one now I can talk to, as of right, without thinking. No one waiting when I come home, nor for whom I

53

wait to tell the small things. The essence of all important things is trivia. I can ring a friend when there is a drama, a crisis, a worry, but who wants my minutiae? – I saw a lovely sunset; a dog ran across the road and I nearly had an accident swerving to avoid it and was frightened.

I cannot remember who said that to tell of your dreams is the highest form of egotism. But it doesn't matter in marriage to say over breakfast: 'I had a nasty dream last night.' When you cannot do that, so easily, the little grey miasma sits in the small of your back for hours.

How was I to know his death would mean a thousand tiny things? Stanley was an excellent speller, and I am hopeless. I couldn't foresee how awkward life would be when I couldn't look across the kitchen table and ask, 'Is tenant spelt "ent" or "ant"? ' Far worse is when I get a tune on my brain, hum it on and off all day, and can only remember half the words, and know Stanley would have known them . . .

There are the practical minutiae, too: my gold chain bracelet came undone and I could not re-clasp it single-handed.

Occasionally, I get a tickle on my back. No longer can I say, 'Scratch it for me, please. A little to the right, up a bit . . . ah, bliss!' I do complicated and rather unhygienic things with the wooden salad fork. I had hiccoughs one night, and suddenly there was no one to give me a drink of water from the wrong side of a glass! I sat miserably, jerking away with a sore diaphragm, and wondered how single people manage!

*

All through our life together, Stanley would occasionally say: 'Loving is needing,' and I disagreed: 'Loving is giving.'

Five months after his death, I broke my ankle. It was just an accident, but I had reached that very vulnerable stage in grieving when you become so absorbed by your internal situation, you overlook ordinary precautions. My accident was simple. I slipped on a cliff path while on holiday and, yet again, within seconds, my whole life changed dramatically.

As I lay spreadeagled under a high, white sky I felt transfixed by God, like a butterfly pinned to paper, and I have never felt so desolate in all my life. Help was only minutes away; the pain was starting to run about like beans in a bean-bag. I was forced to do what I had been avoiding for months, to reach down inside myself, deep, deep, to see if I had some essential grit, and guts, and strength. I turned over and began to crawl up the muddy slope on hands and knees.

In the hotel, where we had spent our last holiday all together, in the ambulance rattling thirty-five miles to hospital, I had never longed for Stanley so much. My last arrogance was gone; loving was indeed needing, he had always given so much. I was so ashamed that I had not before realised how much he gave. Had he been there, he would have been in a panic; he hated me to change my hair, to wear a hat, to be different, to be ill. He would have concealed all his emotions, and I would have been able to make light of my distress. I would have held his hand, as he would have held my hand, and when the shock and pain had lessened, we would have laughed, made a good story of it.

That accident taught me a good deal. I had been afraid, wondering how I would manage, living alone. I learned I did not need to be afraid. I learned to ask for help, not to be afraid of fear, not to be too proud, to rely on the great wealth of kindness in the world.

Such family as I have, my friends and neighbours rallied to help me. They poured into the house, to shop for me, walk the dogs, drive me about, to chat. By the curious inter-penetration of opposites, when I was most alone, I had most company.

Before, I had always feared isolation and loneliness, run from it, filled up my life with trivials and over-work. When I was confronted with the fear, face-to-face, it vanished.

Stanley and I had often discussed the question of loneliness. After he died, I went on discussing it with him. This was not morbid, a denial that he was not there, a Miss Haversham act, but an act of love and faith.

Life goes on, death is a continuum, but life well lived and death well accepted is the best tribute and memorial to someone you love deeply.

The break was an extremely bad one, and for months I was in pain and discomfort. All my attention was concentrated on practical things; how to get in and out of a chair, to reach a lavatory, to dress and undress. Because, by then, I spoke freely to Stanley in my mind, I said, 'You've taken second place to a broken ankle, I'm afraid. What a thing!' and I could see him smile.

Curiously, the pain gave me a holiday from myself, helped my emotions to heal. Just before the accident, I had entered a bad phase of grieving. I felt I was going to disintegrate completely. I feared I should turn into a tramp; not bothering to wash, wearing layers of odd clothes, living over hot-air vents with my feet in cardboard boxes. There would be no one to stop me, and I would go beyond the state of being able to stop myself. Perhaps a broken ankle was a small price to pay!

*

In the casualty ward of our local hospital, a nurse came to ask if I would like a cup of tea while waiting for transport home. We looked at each other, knew we had met. We chatted, trying to find the connection. Finally, memory came shambling through the obscuring mists. I could see her walking towards me, how her fringe bobbed up and down, and I exclaimed: 'At Easter!' as she called my husband by his name, remembered him and remembered me. We talked about him, perfectly naturally. She had no coy inhibitions

56

about mentioning the dead. We discussed the other people in his ward; they were Stanley's and my last 'mutual friends'. When I needed him so badly, I felt just as if he had reached out his hand and covered mine, as he so often used to do: 'Are you all right, my sweetie?'

I found I had sowed seeds of other, secret, flowers, but sometimes they are invisible.

*

Everyone who grieves is alike. I may have missed some phases – and they are only phases – others have experienced. They, in turn, will identify immediately: 'That's me, that's just what I felt!'

Probably the most universal, most traumatic and hardest phase is the state of remorse. Second only to this is the feeling that it is all a mistake, the death has not happened, a magic wand will wave and we shall wake from the walking nightmare, go back to the times before.

This is a form of madness. We all fear madness, but it is present in the hidden heart of all grief. Personally, I found it better to accept this, be first cousin to King Lear, than to deny it. My brain and intellect said one thing; my heart, my emotions another. If there is no point of reconciliation, this must be madness.

I knew Stanley was dead. I had been with him less than an hour before he died. I had wondered, briefly – and there must be few who have not wondered this – if it was only an empty coffin at the cremation.

And then I became gripped by a wild and passionate conviction that I should find him again. There were days when every time the phone rang I was filled by an exultant, terrifying certainty that when I lifted the receiver I should hear his very deep, distinctive voice saying my name. I felt that if I rang the office, he would answer me.

For weeks, against all reason, I felt that if I went back to the hospice, I should find him there, sitting small and white in his chair, his hollowed blue eyes watching for me.

It was the most horrifying experience I have ever had. There was no help, there was nothing I could do. The misery was a physical pain, so bad I simply sat in my chair, rocking back and forth, tears pouring down my face.

I was a bitch in the woodland, howling beside the dead body of her master, returning again and again, slipping a collar at night.

It took months to pass completely. It was essential to talk, to find someone – priest, friend, stranger – to take up my courage, say the words, cry the tears.

My help came from an acquaintance, a neighbour. In her house, I knew I had to find the courage, overcome my deep inhibitions and shyness, let the mumbled words come stumbling out. It was the hardest thing I have ever done in my life; the emotion I now know to be so common seemed so unnatural, and every inhibition and every barrier in my mind screamed, 'Don't say it,' because I really feared I was going mad. In a rush I said, 'I keep thinking he's still there, and I'll find him if I go back!'

She was so calm and uncurious, I felt a violent wave of irrational anger, as well as relief.

But it made the second and third time I needed to tell it to others much easier. When I reached that 'Beechers Brook' again, it had shrunk to a low brush fence, and I could talk about it naturally, until I did not need to tell it any more.

A neighbour told me how her father died. 'And your mother? How did she manage?' She was crisp: 'She bottled all her feelings up inside herself, doubled her smoking and died a year later.'

But I have work to do, responsibilities. I feel myself recovering, as if from a long illness; upsurges in vitality, what Stanley used to call, 'Your driving, restless energy; you give no peace to yourself, or to anyone else!'

My daughter and I went back to the places where we had

last been with him. I drove past the hospital, round the side road where I used to park, full to over-flowing with the feeling that he was still there, that if I went in through the wide doors, up the stone staircase beneath the glass dome, I should still find him in his chair, by the corner bed under the high window.

Even doing that made me less safe to drive than if I had drunk two double whiskies. Tears made the traffic lights splinter, and all the street lamps turn to variegated colours.

I drove by the hospice, looked at the window where I had stood that last morning, and I saw the reversed view. It was very painful, but I felt I had to do this. I think it helped, but I do not understand how or why.

My daughter, so much her father's child, braver by far than I, actually went to the hospital, walked down the long corridor between the wards, glanced in at 'his' bed. It was at least six months later before I was able to do this. I was away when she visited the hospital. I should probably have tried to stop her had I known; perhaps that was why she chose to go then, perhaps she had her own wisdom. She paid a heavy price, with a recurrence of the nervous rash down her spine which she developed after her father's death. But, as he died in his own way, so people must live in their own way, follow their own secret stars, sow their own secret flowers.

*

The remorse – and who has not felt it after a death? – was worse; the most unpleasant thing I have ever experienced. I was attacked by memory. I realised how often I must have wounded his feelings, and I now realised how the hurt had been done casually and unconsciously; my indifference and self-absorption; my lack of understanding and petty resentments. I was often hard, antagonistic and unforgiving.

I thought of our rows. Although we disliked being in

contention with each other, he was always more ready with a gracious apology than I. And now it was too late to say 'Sorry', to put things right.

The unhappiness and guilt went round and round in my mind. I thought I was going mad, and perhaps I did.

I had to do something. I had to think hard, and quickly. This is my conclusion.

I had indeed hurt him, brushed his feelings to one side, and since I could not have time back to undo them, I must abide by the consequences of my deeds, and I must accept this, because there was no alternative. But that this pain might not be sterile, I must hope to learn, so that in my future relationships I do not make the same mistakes – or not so often. I must use this time and this pain constructively, so that it be not wasted.

I was helped very much by my daughter, to whom I confided some of these feelings – and I found that difficult because we had changed places; it was she who was reassuring me. While Stanley was ill, at home, I bought him an expensive present. He was very indifferent, although I now realise it was because he was so much more seriously ill than I had known. But at the time, I was upset and he knew it. Anne repeated what he had said when I had left the room: 'Oh, dear, I've hurt her, and I didn't mean to. The trouble is, I'm never very good at saying how much I love her.' And, of course, I forgave the hurt at once, as he forgave me. He must have done, otherwise we would not have been able to live together; that was the proof.

And, in forgiving him, I learned to forgive myself.

*

I turned the situation upside down. I wondered how Stanley would have managed, what he would have felt, what he would have missed most about me if I had died first. I remember a boy-friend of Anne's saying to me, 'The light really goes out of this house when you are away.'

I was seldom away for more than a night or two, and although Stanley never said anything, I knew he minded. Until five months after his death, I had never done what he had done, spent a night alone in the house where I now live permanently alone.

I smiled, thinking to myself, knowing some of the things Stanley would have found most difficult. No one but I has ever been able to work the washing-machine, and certainly no one else has ever understood the central heating and its time clock!

I regained some balance and self-confidence, a little self-esteem.

*

I miss the little treats. We never had much money, but occasionally Stanley would say, 'Let's all go out for dinner,' and we went to our cheap, favourite local restaurant, where we always went on birthdays. Now, there is no one to say that. I miss saying, 'When you come to think of Christmas presents, such-and-such would be very acceptable.' I miss being petted and cosseted; the flowers or chocolates, rare but always fun. I can buy them, of course, but it is not the same. Now there is no one to bring me a cup of tea, cook dinner if I come home exhausted. And when I have made a particularly successful deal in my business, there is no one to whom I can readily say, 'Life has given me a little bonus. Let's go and celebrate.' And Stanley would let me stand us all a dinner or a theatre.

One day, showing him some goods I had bought, I said, 'I'm very lucky,' and he replied, 'You work very hard and consistently. You make your own good luck.' This is a remark I treasure as a talisman.

Although I lived for years as part of a family, in a house often full of guests and visitors, I spent – and spend – a good deal of time alone. Before we knew he was ill, I was irritable. I would ask Stanley to do small chores, be cross when they were not done. I remember thinking, 'I'm being trained to be a widow.'

*

It has taken me many months to begin to rebuild my self-confidence. I have, after all, been left and deserted. He may not have wished to go, but he has gone. He has left me; not for another woman, but for another life. I have gone straight back to the shyness, the insecurity and inadequacies of the most painful stage of adolescence, not made any easier by the fact that it is familiar, I have been through this before.

People say, 'I'd like my youth back,' but they do not really think what this means.

I have had it back. I would not recommend it.

As an adolescent has to do – break through the bud of childhood, open the petals and find themselves – as I did forty years ago, so I had to do again, to remake myself, to rebuild my life.

To begin with, it was utterly exhausting; to start things, to take the initiative, to telephone someone and ask them for a meal. All I wanted to do was to sit back and be passive, to wait until I was invited out, and then, when I was asked to go somewhere, I didn't want to go. Now, months afterwards, I still have to be asked twice, even by people close to me, to be really sure they want me.

I realised from chatting to another widow that I could not ask strangers into the house, and it was I who kept my new acquaintance at arm's length. All the people who came to my home were old friends. I became very uneasy when a new friend called.

But now, when someone comes to stay, I enjoy them for themselves and not because they fill the empty gaps in my big house. When they leave, and I hold them a second time for yet another hug, another kiss, it is only because I love them, not because I want to keep them. We meet cleanly, on an equal footing; they, because they want to come to see me, and I, simply because I enjoy seeing them for themselves.

Naturally, I love above all else to see my daughter, to hear her news and doings. But I do not have to live vicariously through her.

I very much appreciated being asked by neighbours to a family dinner one Sunday evening. Our children have been friends since they were at primary school; we have a long, comfortable, casual relationship. I didn't feel prickly, as I sometimes did with other people, who made me feel that they were 'being kind'. People said, 'You must come round for a meal, we'll fix it sometime.' I have said this myself, and until I was a brand-new widow, I never understood the hurt and rejection when they didn't 'fix it'.

Does everyone have my irritable pride? It was enormously important to have the luxury of refusing an invitation, to say, 'I'm so very sorry I can't come, because . . .', to appear to be much in demand socially! I had to put up a front to everyone, to my daughter, and even to myself, that I was independent and all right, but as I walked with daily emotional footsteps, I knew the crust was very thin and the threat of total internal disintegration frighteningly real.

*

I must have learned something in the years of 'belonging', something to help in my relationships now that I do not 'belong'. The thirty years of knowing my husband has given me something, and changed me, so that I do not really need to be afraid that I shall go back to my unhappy, insecure younger self. I have drawn heavily, therefore, on the bank of happy days. But every relationship, no matter how old and tried, had to be re-tested, re-established. Some were exactly the same, others are now different. Some friends are new – the beginnings of affection and respect with people Stanley did not know.

I am touched by affection – and this is dangerous, it lacks a balance and makes me vulnerable and afraid. I had to go out among people, do things that if I still had a husband alive I should not be bothered with. I felt, therefore, that things I did were second-rate. I was humiliated, and despised myself for this, and these feelings stopped me extracting what pleasure was there to be gained.

But gradually, it smoothed out. I now see this whole area of my life with more normality. I have not yet made close, new friendships, but I can move among people I like, whom I find companionable. But it was not easy to force myself out of my cave.

*

I was determined that no one should pity us. Savagely, I resisted this. Sympathy, that Anne and I welcomed; under-standing and kindness, too, but pity, no. I watched other people with on-going lives and changing interests; I did not want to be left behind, on a shelf. I had no energy or drive to join in the main stream, indeed, I had only just enough to keep on with my outward pattern of life, but I did not wish to be left in a backwater.

I said to Anne, 'Each week, we must make a little celebration, give ourselves a treat. We'll go to a theatre, a cinema, go out for a meal. There are times when you have to spend money – usually when you can least afford to!' No one was going to say we had lost all interest in life; we had to put on a good face for the world. Yet I had a great fear that acquaintances might see us at a theatre and say to themselves, 'Mary's enjoying herself! Hasn't she got over her husband's death quickly!'

The time for crying in public had gone, the time for crying in private had arrived.

*

At first, I cried every day. There was nothing I could do to stop the easy tears. Then I would find I had gone through a whole day without crying, and I panicked; had I got over his death too soon? Never believe there is not madness in grief! I had a pattern soon; one day of crying followed by a day when tears were unobtainable and nothing I could think would make me cry. The internal wound ached and ached, but when I laughed, and I did laugh, often, I feared most that people would think I did not care.

*

With my own father, I had a clear, untroubled relationship. I was never jealous of the love between my husband and his daughter; their relationship was close and, therefore, at times exclusive. I used to say, 'Any daughter worth her salt should be able to wrap her father round her little finger. I could mine!' Our love did not stop my father pulling me up short if I stepped out of line: 'I don't really care for that sort of behaviour, poppet.'

Now, there is no one to correct me if I go astray; if unwittingly I cause hurt and affront; nothing except that early training and the conditioning of my years of marriage. I am accountable to no one. I am dangerous, I am rogue. Although I still give love and affection, there is almost nobody I care for desperately, above all others, and therefore nobody from whom I would accept discipline, and nobody who has a right to give it. I am frightened of myself. To me, this is one of the inner hearts of grieving. I am alone. I identify that loneliness. I must accustom myself to it.

*

Those who are bereaved must, without any question, walk with loneliness. Family, friends, society, circle round me, loving and concerned, but wary and at a distance.

Loneliness is the halitosis of the soul; instantly recognised, politely not mentioned. Only one friend asked, forthrightly, 'Do you find Sundays difficult?'

For the first time in my life I lied, consistently and deliberately. Before long, I believed the lie: 'I like being on my own.' I no longer know where the truth begins and the fiction ends.

Like many people, I have had occasion to visit houses where misery and loneliness are palpable, like the lingering smell of boiled cabbage, and I have turned away, flinching from the unspoken, emotional demand. I did not want people to turn from me, especially at a time when I needed them so much, and so I lied to protect myself.

I tried to cut the situation down to size, to turn loneliness into just a ten-letter word. I made it smaller, into an eight-letter word, and called it solitude. Whatever it was, I knew I could not defeat it, so I fought a guerrilla war. One of my weapons – although I was not quite so light-hearted as Belloc's Lady Poltagrue – was to make use of solitude, make it a time to think and consider and reflect.

For years and years, we had been so busy living and doing, we never had time to pause. Life had been like a rabbit, hopping ahead of us, and we, our eyes fixed on its scut, bobbed along behind, pausing to scrabble and find money to pay the bills, deal with the family problems, recharge our batteries with a brief rest on holiday. Now, I had an opportunity for peace, the cloister time of tranquillity.

I thought of our life together, the home we had made. I had a big house to run as well as a business, and there was the school routine, meals and a constant stream of guests. Within five months, that life vanished; my husband was dead, my daughter gone away to college.

To sit in misery would deny everything we had ever done together, throw it all away as worthless, would kill and deny some essence of Stanley that still lives in me, more surely than death and the cancers had done. And it would be I who had killed that spirit, by a self-absorption in my own transient emotion. And I should atrophy, perhaps my own driving life-force would wither and die.

I looked at the house: worn carpets, because most of them had been bought second-hand, and shabby chair covers where the cats sharpen their claws and the dogs sit, despite my constant nagging. But it is a house full of sunlight and books; we put up shelf after shelf, in every room, and there are still not enough. It is a home full of music; someone would pass the piano and play for ten minutes before a meal was ready, or play for hours on end because they wanted to do so. Records, too; pop music upstairs often competing with classical music downstairs. And chat, endless talk and gossip, mostly trivial, some serious, and laughter, so that whoever lives here in the future will be happy, because the laughter has soaked into the walls.

I made the garden, with happy ignorance, choosing only plants I knew and liked; soft colours and sweet scents. I remember one summer morning, waiting for the family to come to breakfast, walking round and talking to my plants; praising those which had done well, admonishing the stunted. I did not know Stanley was sitting in the kitchen, listening. He grinned up at me. 'You know, one day one of those flowers will answer you back, and that'll make you think!'

I could not, could not, throw all this away because I was selfish, concerned only with a pain which must be temporary.

So, I forced grief to give me time to think.

After birth, animals go into a quiet corner with their young, plenty of 'cave time'. Nature makes the bereaved need to be alone – however terrifying it is – to heal.

I had, in truth, to say: 'Do not fear loneliness, nor call it by another name. It is necessary.'

*

For a long time, I felt as if there were two halves of me; an outside and an inside, and they had no connection with each other, but slipped about like steel plates with broken rivets. Very slowly, the two halves are joining together normally, and I no longer feel so odd, so de-personalized.

I have been through so much, too quickly. I am a new person, and I do not know that person yet. I am wary, suspicious and a little scared of myself. I do not quite trust the person I now am, and I wonder if Stanley will recognise me when we meet again, since I do not really recognise myself.

I feel this new person is much harder, more ruthless. The selfishness I tried to eliminate in my marriage has returned and been reinforced. I have a childish wilfulness: 'I don't *have* to do anything!' I have had to fight so hard to find a little firm ground for my feet, a little patch of sunlight to stand in, that I cannot let other people's wants and needs affect me. Whether there are other people staying in the house or not, I lead my own life in exactly the same way. I put out clean sheets, but I don't bother to make up the beds.

*

A couple of years before Stanley died, I went to do a course of evening classes. I had waited a long time to have the leisure and energy for this study. It was as if my guardian angel watched for me, because here were the seeds of a new interest, a new way of life, new contacts, even friends. The classes were pleasant and absorbing. I said at home, 'I don't think about you, the house, the business, any problems. When I am there, it's the only time I am ever unfaithful.'

But life has made me unfaithful – and perhaps even death has tried to do so as well and that is why I resent it. I am not the same person as I was. In the past months, so much has happened that Stanley does not know about, although he would have been immensely interested. I have been taken away, too.

And yet the reality of him is so close that momentarily I get muddled, and sometimes think, for example, my broken ankle happened long before, not months after, he died.

I am in no way the person who stood in the X-ray clinic, heard the sister ask, 'Did you know he has a lump?' and knew it for what it proved to be.

There have been a million things we would have talked about; unshared, each one has been an act of separation.

I do not know what happened to Stanley, what he thought or felt, in those last three weeks, although I saw him twice a day. There was no way I could know; I could only make an informed guess occasionally. His form of illness made a change, a qualitative leap into a new dimension, from which there was no point of return. We could never discuss it.

Stanley and I did not want to leave each other, but we had to do so.

Oh, yes, sorrows mark you!

*

Of course, I have 'seen' him since he died. I am not going to put my head on the chopping block of contention and say it was actually my dead husband. I retain my private conviction and opinion. But what I saw was so vivid: sun shining on his hair, the high-necked jersey that Stanley favoured, dark sports jacket, grey trousers. The man was standing on the kerb, waiting for a gap in the traffic and easing his shoulders back with the typical, unconscious gesture of a bronchitic.

From the window one night, from the corner of my eye, I saw the broad shoulders and camel-hair coat, and wondered why he walked across the road and not up the front steps.

Otherwise, I do not 'see' him; I become frightened because I cannot picture him, remember exactly what he looked like – the face I saw daily, changing over thirty years.

To begin with, the family photo album was unbearable, then an endless joy. In that slow record of time, he looks happier as the years go on. I have no photos of him in the rooms. When I do occasionally see one of him – pinned up by his daughter in her college room – it gives me a shock; it looks so like him! Very slowly – and for some reason I do not understand I find this of immense importance – I am remembering him for myself. Small details: how his hair grew, the different coloured greys in it; the shape of his brilliantly blue eyes that are echoed in his daughter and two of his sons; the shape of his hands.

*

I was so glad, so very glad, of the letters. I gathered a small treasury of the things people said, the anecdotes, the repeated remarks. Letters comforted, and meant that, even for five minutes only, someone had thought of us, had bothered to show they cared. They helped enormously in that early limbo land, even those letters which spoke of the desolation, and also told me it would pass. I did not believe them, but they were right; it does get better. One very old friend sent a 90-minute tape from abroad. It said: 'Stanley was so brave. He would have made a fine soldier.' Without thinking, I knew it was true. I had always known it, but why had I never consciously recognised it?

And how I now miss that soldier, and only now realise that we fought shoulder to shoulder. He must have found it a relief not to be alone; I am comforted that, unconsciously, I gave him that comradeship. Like characters from a saga, we covered each other's back, and now that his shield is hung up on the wall, I miss him.

Occasionally, we turned our fighting talents on each other, which caused some memorable scenes. I still remember the satisfaction when I threw a cup of tea over him! No point in pretending it didn't happen; it was part of us.

All these things helped to round out a picture of the man I had lost; lost inside myself, because in those early days of grief I walked with a desolation I had never guessed existed. I could not remember him for what he had been. The letters, the stories re-drew the cartoon outline for me. But the people I really valued were the ones who were brave enough to tell me something.

His favourite cousin, so shy and inhibited, said, 'He always loved you so much for making him laugh!' and I carried that remark, like a child with a treasured pebble, in my hand for days. From my own experience, I know her to be of kind intelligence and high integrity. Were these things not so, my husband would never have accorded her so much affection. But it is a measure of my own unbalanced state of mind that at the time I wondered if she were 'primed' to relate that remark.

Another friend told me of an incident on holiday. She and Stanley watched me chat to a stranger on the beach, and Stanley said of me, 'That's what I love so much about her, her ready warmth and ability to talk to people. I can never do that.'

Two people said little, simply asked me for a photo of him; I was so touched. In the very early days, I had a brief but

71

violent complex that I must smell of the grave. So much of me had gone, how could it not be so? But all these little things helped to give him back to me, and to give me back to myself.

*

My small reading on the business of grief tells of the sudden, unexpected feeling of closeness. I have known that, too.

Two days after his death, going to the bank for dreary business details, I felt him walking beside me. I was filled with a great, exultant joy. It only happens occasionally. I am a gnomon, I show only the happy hours. I sing with delight, I feel even the backs of my ears are smiling. He is in my mind almost all the time. He was during life, so why should mere death change the habit?

Months later, a business friend said, 'You two were always so intimate, so conscious of each other, it's not surprising you're so desolate.' But I was surprised. I had not realised, and therefore had not realised that it showed. We smiled together and I recited the Arab proverb: 'There are three things that cannot be hid; love, smoke, and a man riding on a camel.'

*

A few months after Stanley died, I visited a very close friend of many years' standing. It seemed so odd to sit in her familiar flat, look at her, talk to her as we have talked out our problems and secrets over more than twenty years. I felt as if I had come back from a long and dangerous journey, had visited a fairy-tale elf-land and returned to the upper world with strange knowledge. I was sad; it was not so much that I would not share it with her, I could not share that knowledge. She will not understand – yet.

I was a little shy when she asked me what it felt like to be a widow, and I looked for words so that she could identify with me. I was only partially successful. I felt inadequate, and also isolated and alone.

On the other hand, I did not wish – though I thought about it – to go to a trained counsellor. I felt this might turn me inward, might reinforce the grieving. I was afraid that counselling would take Stanley away from me. The fact that death had actually done so already I quite ignored. I am absolutely sure that this is not true for everyone; that counselling is a complete lifeline and necessity, but I personally was lucky: in my friends, in being able to make myself talk, to leave matters to time and let nature take its course, to learn to listen to my body, to cry as I must, to heal in my own way.

*

Despite all the pain, the agony and tears, I know now that above all these things I am lucky. That tiresome little quotation jogged into my mind, ''Tis better to have loved and lost . . .'* I kept stubbing a mental toe against that cliché, and the truth in it. Many, many people have a secret, warped – and perhaps justified – fear that they are incapable of love.

To my own immense surprise – because there was nothing in my somewhat chequered early life to indicate this – I find now that I am a one-man woman.

Death, and the aftermath of devastating grief, has put all sorts of things into perspective. Death has given me one priceless gift, that of knowing I did love; once; deeply and truly. So I am safe, now and for ever.

* Alfred, Lord Tennyson, *In Memoriam A.H.H.*

73

It has always been a cause of embarrassment to me that I cry easily. The family would tease me. Sunsets, music, poetry, all set me off. I can see Stanley now, and his alarmed concern as I watched something on the television: 'Are you crying, or seriously crying, or just crying with laughter?' How he hated me to cry! But, when I had to do so, tears were my great safety valve.

In the bad days, I walked daily with the dogs, blind with tears. Twice, the pain came down like a pulsing, red under-skin over my eyes. It was like tremendous anger, literally seeing red, a second in which to commit murder. Sometimes, the tears were easy and left me clear-eyed, sparkling and pretty; sometimes they were so hard I was puffy and plain, red and swollen for hours afterwards. I did not know any one person could have so many tears inside them.

I remembered my first job – I was seventeen – and the light-hearted nonsense of another girl: 'I cried so much, I used up all that week's ration of tears!'

*

I have kept my word. The ribbon is now fading.

*

In these few months, I have thought many things, seen many pictures in my mind's eye. The last came as my ankle was healing, the broken bones joining invisibly, taking their own mysterious time under the plaster, inside my skin.

I saw Stanley and me as one of those pencil-sharpeners, shaped as a globe. Two separate halves that were meaning-less; blue for the sea, squiggles marking land and rivers. But each half was threaded. Useless alone, put together they made sense, joining seas and continents, completing names, a perfect whole, no seam showing, no crack for the fingernail, a picture of the world.

CODA

A friend from New York wrote: 'It would be interesting to know how you re-built your life.' I gave an instant, internal, scream of pain: 'But I haven't rebuilt it.'

However, struggling to be honest, I now think the pencil-sharpener is the penultimate picture, and the most recent one is of me as a bushy plant, pruned back down to the roots, and through the dead wood, new shoots grow, strong stems and fragile leaves.

One time, between sleep and waking, between dark and dawning, a finger tapped my shoulder, and a voice full of kindness said, 'You must turn your back on him and walk away. You have always known you would have to do this.'

So, Stanley is only an incident – prolonged and profound, but only an incident, an interlude in my life?

But I wasn't obedient. I am wilful; I like my own way.

I remembered when we quarrelled so violently we had to have a third person present to stop us going for the jugular, yet we never turned our backs on each other. So how can I do this now, go walking away, whistling into the sunrise? How can I not, since everything I have written is a denial of death, which I do not understand, and since I am realistic and death is the most undeniable fact in the world.

The end is as it was at the end. Stanley is in my mind and my heart, and I am me and we are still part of each other. And so we will go on again – together. But at the end of the day, when I am tired, what I miss is his hand on mine. The blood courses warm under my skin, and it does not do so under his.

All I do know, poor fool and jackanapes that I am, is that not until the last few pages of typing this did it occur to me that I have written a love story.

And that I, like you, the reader, have to make the best of this that I can.

USEFUL ADDRESSES

CRUSE: Bereavement Care, Cruse House, 126 Sheen Road, Richmond TW9 1UR, 01 940 4818/9047.

Age Concern is developing bereavement counselling in some of its areas and can give much general support to the elderly. They also have a wide range of fact sheets on practical problems facing the elderly, especially housing.

Age Concern England: Bernard Sunley House, 60 Pitcairn Road, Mitcham, Surrey, 01 640 5431.
Age Concern Scotland: 33 Castle Street, Edinburgh EH2 3DW, 031 225 5000.
Age Concern Wales: 1 Park Grove, Cardiff, S. Glamorgan, 0222 371566.
Age Concern N. Ireland: 129 Great Victoria Street, Belfast BT2 7BG, 0232 245729.

AIDS. For counselling and advice telephone *Terrence Higgins Trust*, 01 833 2971; Welsh AIDS Campaign, 0222 464121; Scottish AIDS Monitor, 031 558 1167.

Foundation for Black Bereaved Families, Lorrene Hunter, 11 Kingston Square, Salters Hill, London SE19, 01 761 7228.

The Foundation for the Study of Infant Deaths, 15 Belgrave Square, London SW1X 8PS, 01 235 1721.

The Secretary is June Reed. There is a contact network
throughout the country to help those bereaved by a cot
death, and information is available on research into the
circumstances of infant death.

Gay Bereavement Project, Unitarian Rooms, Hoop
Lane, London NW11 8BS, 01 455 8894.
Offers help to lesbians and gay men whose partners
have died, especially in the first difficult hours and days
of bereavement.
London Lesbian and Gay Switchboard 01 837 7324 can
put caller in touch with a volunteer.

Hospice Information Service, St. Christopher's
Hospice, 51–9 Lawrie Park Road, Sydenham, London
SE26 6DZ, 01 778 1240.
The Hospice Movement provides care for adults who
are terminally ill. There is also a hospice for children
which gives parents a break if they are caring for
terminally ill children. This is Helen House, 37 Leopold
Street, Oxford OX4 1QT, 0865 728251.

National Association for Widows, Neville House,
Waterloo Street, Birmingham, 021 643 8348.
Offers self help and friendship to widows and
campaigns vigorously for benefits and a better statutory
deal for widows. Branches nationwide.

Parents of Murdered Children (part of Society of
Compassionate Friends), c/o Anne Robinson, 10
Eastern Avenue, Prittlewell, Southend on Sea, Essex
SS2 5QU, 0702 68510.

SANDS (Stillbirth and Neonatal Death Society), 28
Portland Place, London W1N 3DE, 01 436 5881.
A self-help group offering understanding and
encouragement to parents bereaved by a stillbirth.

Society of Compassionate Friends, Head Office: 6
Denmark Street, Bristol BS1 5DQ, 0272 292778.
An international organisation of bereaved parents
offering friendship and understanding to other
bereaved parents. There is a county secretary for most
counties, and contact information can be obtained
through the National Secretary.